D1117680

Cupcakes for Christmas

Cupcakes for Christmas

A Return to Willoughby Close Romance

KATE HEWITT

TULE
PUBLISHING

Cupcakes for Christmas
Copyright© 2018 Kate Hewitt
Tule Publishing First Printing, September 2018

The Tule Publishing Group, LLC

ALL RIGHTS RESERVED

First Publication by Tule Publishing Group 2018

No part of this book may be used or reproduced in any manner
whatsoever without written permission except in the case of brief
quotations embodied in critical articles and reviews.

This is a work of fiction. Names, characters, places, and incidents are
products of the author's imagination or are used fictitiously. Any
resemblance to actual events, locales, organizations, or persons, living or
dead, is entirely coincidental.

ISBN: 978-1-949707-07-6

Chapter One

"HEY, OLIVIA!"

Olivia James looked up from her shopping list with a smile for twelve-year-old Mallory Lang as, on a gust of cold air, she breezed into Tea on the Lea, the tea shop Olivia had been running for the last two years.

Mallory shook her long, blonde hair over her shoulders as she collapsed into one of the white wrought-iron chairs at a small, spindly table and shivered dramatically. "It's freezing out there. Mum says it might snow."

"A white Christmas? That would be lovely." Olivia came around the counter to close the door a bit more firmly; it really was cold, and her little shop's antiquated bow windows were not double-glazed. Although it was only a little past three, outside the sky was already turning to the colour of pewter and only a few brave souls were walking down Wychwood-on-Lea's high street, heads tucked low against the chilly December wind.

"Have you got something for me to try?" Mallory asked with pseudo-nonchalance, still sometimes trying to play the cool kid even though Olivia knew her far too well for that. During the two years since she'd moved to Wychwood-on-Lea, she'd become good friends with Mallory's mother, Harriet, as well as the other three residents of Willoughby Close, a courtyard of converted-stables cottages on the grounds of Willoughby Manor. Harriet and her neighbours Ellie, Ava, and Alice regularly came in to the shop for coffees and chat, and more often than not Olivia pulled up a chair and joined them.

It had been a lovely surprise to find unexpected friends in a village where a single woman pushing forty was considered a bona fide spinster, someone who should invest in a plaid wheelie bag and a tabby cat. Although now, thanks to her mum moving into retired housing two months ago, she was in possession of the latter—a massive, marmalade, and monstrous beast aptly named Dr Jekyll.

"Indeed I do have something for you to try," Olivia told Mallory. "Another cupcake." Since Mallory had started secondary school a little over a year ago, she'd been coming into the shop every so often and hanging out for an hour or so before heading home. She'd even started bringing friends along on occasion, so that Tea on the Lea was turning into Wychwood-on-Lea's cool destination for tweens, not that they had many options.

Besides a couple of pubs and a charity shop, the village nestled next to the Lea River in England's rolling Cotswolds had very few retail possibilities. Teenagers tended to hang about the village green or the skate park, looking vaguely menacing in their dark hoodies, phones practically pressed to their faces. Far better for them to be in here, scoffing scones and fizzy drinks, which Olivia now stocked in a chilling cabinet for expressly that purpose.

It had been a steep learning curve, taking over her mother's tea shop six months ago, after having helped her out for a year and a half before that. Tina James was a fantastic baker and a not-so-good business owner, by her own cheerful admission. She simply hadn't cared about money, never had, preferring to bake and chat, to listen and love, running the shop like her own kitchen, and relying on a double mortgage to keep her afloat.

Olivia had been working tirelessly, trying to boost the little shop's custom as well as the services and goods it offered. Hence, the cupcakes, as well as the new website, the made-to-order wedding cake service, the venue-for-hire option, and the Mums' Morning Out she offered once a week, with a box of toys in the corner, and a special two-for-one offer on muffins.

Now Olivia took out her latest creation, made early that morning, when the world had still been pitch black, the winter dawn hours in the offing, the little shop freezing as the pipes clanked and the heat slowly began to kick in.

"My cookies and cream cupcake," she announced, and placed it in front of Mallory with a flourish. "Chocolate cake and vanilla buttercream icing, with cookie pieces on top," she added. "Give me your honest opinion."

Olivia stood back, her hands on her hips, as Mallory took a big bite. One of her more recent initiatives—only in the last few days, as a matter of fact—had been to start offering cupcakes—gorgeous, fluffy, decadent cakes the size of your fist, loaded up with icing and decorated to perfection, a step up from the scones and sponge cake she usually offered, and when placed in the shop's front bow window in a tantalising display, hopefully enough to entice a passer-by into the shop—and to make a purchase or two.

"This is *amazing*," Mallory gushed as she wiped a dab of icing from her upper lip. "The chocolate is so gooey and yummy." She hesitated, and Olivia's eyes narrowed.

"But…?"

"But maybe it could use a few more cookie pieces on top? Not just for decoration, but you know, because, *yum?*"

"Yum. Okay." Olivia nodded, smiling. She'd be lavish with the Oreos; why not? If you were going to treat yourself to a ginormous cupcake, best to make it—and the calories—worth your while. "And that's why I need you to test them, Mallory." She made a note to order more cookies along with everything else for her weekly shop on Sunday, after she visited her mum in her retirement flat in Witney.

"You know what you should do?" Mallory said, her words a bit garbled around another mouthful of cupcake. Olivia glanced up from her notepad, waiting for Mallory to swallow—and stop spraying crumbs. Her glance moved around the little shop, with its old oak counter, six tables crammed quite close together, the wrought-iron shelving unit bedecked with boxes of macaroons and vintage teacups for sale. Three weeks before Christmas and she needed to start decorating—both cakes and the shop.

She'd go all out for Christmas as she always did, with fairy lights and evergreen boughs, and red velvet bows to match her red velvet cupcakes. She was even thinking of running a mulled-wine-and-mince-pies evening this year, opening the shop at night, fairy lights twinkling among the holly. She could invite her friends, and if they invited their other friends, and Harriet did her usual trick of asking all the schools mums, it could be quite a nice crowd, and hopefully make a decent profit.

"Hmm? What is it that I should do?" she asked as Mallory swallowed the last bit of cupcake and shot a quick but longing glance at the Victorian cake stand on the counter, with two pieces of lemon drizzle and one of Victoria sponge left.

"You could do a promotion around the cupcakes!" she said, turning away from the cake stand to give Olivia the full force of her bright blue eyes and wide, engaging smile. "You have so many fab flavours—what was yesterday's?"

"German chocolate." With a dusting of coconut and a glacé cherry on top. Olivia had been quite proud of those, and had managed to sell five.

"And mint chocolate chip before that, and then lemon

raspberry... Why don't you make a different flavour every day? You could have the Twelve Days of Cupcakes!"

"The Twelve Days of Cupcakes..." Olivia mulled this over for a moment, intrigued. It would be fairly challenging to make a differently flavoured cupcake every day, but it could work if she only made a dozen...limited edition, if you like. And for the person who bought a cupcake on each day, she'd offer a free one at the end. Encourage repeat purchasing, or so the book she'd been reading like it held the answers to life, *Fail-Safe Marketing for the Small Business*, recommended. "That's a good idea, Mallory," she said finally. "I might just do it. I don't think I've actually made twelve different flavours yet, though."

"You can come up with others easy, I bet." Mallory whipped out her phone with its sparkly, rhinestone-encrusted case, her thumbs flying over the screen. "Here you go...Nutella swirl cupcakes, *yum*...strawberry lemonade ones...cherry Coke...not sure about that one, actually. Sounds a bit revolting, but *still*. There are loads of others."

She brandished the phone towards Olivia and she squinted—she was used to a rather larger font—and scrolled down the list. Cherry cheesecake...chocolate peanut butter...salted caramel...they all looked scrumptious. And weren't cupcakes still a thing? She'd read about cupcake bakeries sprouting up all over the place, from New York to London to Tokyo. What if she made it her specialty? A Tea on the Lea cupcake. People would come to the village specifically to buy one. Perhaps she could get a write-up in *Cotswold Life*…

"They do look rather good," she told Mallory. "I'll have to try some of those out."

"So you'll do it?"

"I'll certainly have a think." It *was* a good idea, even if the prospect of adding another item to her to-do list, coming up with crazy confections each and every day, was a bit daunting. Already she had to wake up well before the crack of dawn to make several batches of muffins and scones as well as three cakes, which were her usual daily offerings in the shop.

She'd started baking the cupcakes on something of a whim, and while it was fun to do something different, between the pair of them, she and Mallory had eaten most of the cakes.

Cupcakes, she'd discovered, were more of an afternoon treat than a morning one, and most of her trade happened in the morning. So far she'd only sold a couple of cupcakes to some harried mums bribing their whingy children on the way back from the school run—yesterday, she recalled guiltily, she'd eaten three herself. They would have gone stale otherwise, and it had saved her from having to make a lonely supper for one.

"I'll certainly think about it," she promised again. "Why don't you take a few back to your family? I'm sure William and Chloe would like one, not to mention your mum and dad."

Olivia loaded four cupcakes into a white pastry box, with *Tea on the Lea* written on the front in curly, silver script. She'd bought a thousand of these boxes in the hopes of having the orders start to pour in, and, admittedly, because she'd got a discount by ordering so many, but right now they were cluttering up her much-needed pantry space and getting precious little use.

"Are you sure? Aren't you going to sell them?"

Olivia shook her head. "Doubtful. It's already getting dark and I'll be lucky if I get a handful of customers for the rest of the day. Plus I made them this morning and they'll go stale by tomorrow." And if she gave them to Mallory, she wouldn't eat them herself. Already comfortably round, she certainly didn't need to start scoffing cupcakes—or three— on a daily basis.

"All right," Mallory said, taking the box. "Thanks, Olivia. But that's even more reason to do the cupcake thing, isn't it—new ones every day since the old ones won't keep." She hoisted her backpack on one skinny shoulder, cocking her finger and thumb at Olivia in a trust-me gesture. "I'm telling you, this is it. Your big break. Will you give me a bonus if you make it big?"

"Unlimited cupcakes for life," Olivia promised. "In whatever flavour you want." Smiling, she watched Mallory flounce out, her phone out and thumbs working madly before the door had closed behind her.

Olivia had known Mallory for nearly two years and she couldn't believe how grown-up she was becoming, half startling maturity, half sulky attitude. Harriet had her hands full, not just with Mallory, but with William, her ten-year-old brother, and Chloe, the family's adorable but slightly spoiled seven-year-old. But then Harriet was one of those frighteningly organised women who didn't seem fazed by anything—or at least she had been, until her life had fallen apart in spectacular style, and then come together again, better than before.

Olivia was happy her friend had found happiness with her husband again—in fact, all four of her friends at Willoughby Close had found their happily-ever-afters, and Olivia had had an admittedly small part to play in each of their stories, whether it was doling out cups of tea and generous slabs of cake, or simply providing a smiling face and a listening ear. Now Ellie and Oliver were married, as were Alice and Henry, and Ava and Jace.

Olivia had made all their wedding cakes, which had brought in a nice bit of business. Since Henry was the local lord of the manor, her cake had been something of a talked-about centrepiece. But wedding cake orders had dropped right off after the summer, and once again Olivia was trying to think of another way to make a go of her little tea shop. At least things were ticking over at the moment…if only just.

Olivia bustled around the shop, tidying up after Mallory and finishing her Christmas shopping list. Darkness was already starting to fall, nearly obscuring the steady trickle of mums and children now coming from the primary school at the top end of the high street. None of them stopped in the shop, and Olivia wasn't surprised. Most mothers just wanted to get home at this point, and the wintry weather would put anyone off lingering in front of the display windows she spent hours trying to make look irresistibly delectable.

Olivia had known when she'd taken on her mum's tea shop that it would be a challenging endeavour. Wychwood-on-Lea was a lovely village, but it was small, and Olivia had always understood that foot traffic alone wouldn't keep the place afloat, something her mum had never seemed to accept. She'd been trying a lot of other strategies, and some had taken off a bit, but things were still tight, and at this point, she thought they might always be.

But that was okay. She sank onto a stool behind the wooden counter, propping her chin in her hands as twilight began to settle softly over the village, the buildings of mellow golden stone becoming shadowy in the darkness.

It was fine. She loved running the tea shop; she loved her friends; she loved Wychwood-on-Lea, its quaint cottages, the river burbling alongside, a soothing balm after the hectic busyness of her London life. Everything was good. Absolutely everything.

The merry jingle of bells on the shop door had Olivia lifting her head, and then quickly standing up as a man came into the shop, ducking his head underneath the stone lintel.

He glanced around the empty space, wrought-iron chairs tucked into tables, everything tidied away.

"I'm sorry…are you still open?"

"Yes, absolutely," Olivia said, widening her welcome smile. "Just a bit slow today… It's so cold, I think everyone wants to get home."

"Completely understandable." He loosened the colourful Dr Who-like scarf from around his neck, glancing at the now rather empty glass display cases with an endearingly boyish interest.

He was, Olivia decided, a most *interesting*-looking man. Tall and lithe, at least six three, she'd say, and a bit gangly and awkward too, in a charming way. When he swung around to look at the display case in front of the counter, his elbow nearly knocked the cake stand but fortunately Olivia whisked it a few inches backwards before he made contact.

He glanced at it, startled, and then gave her a sheepish smile. "Sorry. I'm horribly clumsy. My mother despaired of me. I managed to break six of her Royal Doulton teacups in one go. Plus saucers."

Olivia gave a little laugh. "And how did you manage that?"

"They were all on a tray and I knocked it with my elbow. Naturally. It was a bridge party, all the ladies of the neighbourhood. She was *not* pleased."

"Oh, dear." Olivia found she couldn't quite look away from his glinting, grey-green eyes and wide, infectious smile.

He had a dimple in one lean cheek, she noticed, which made him look boyish, although the streaks of grey in his dark, unruly hair, as well as the deepening crow's feet by his eyes suggested someone close to her age of nearly forty.

"Anyway." He glanced up from the display case, eyebrows raised. "What do you recommend?"

"Umm…I'm afraid there's not much left. All the scones are gone, as well as the triple chocolate cake. It's only lemon drizzle or Victoria sponge on offer now…" Her gaze fell on the last cookies and cream cupcake. "Or a cupcake, if you'd rather. I have one left."

His face lit up, making her laugh at the exuberance of his expression. "One cupcake left? How perfectly serendipitous. What flavour is it?"

"Cookies and cream." She fetched the cupcake from the plate behind her; she hadn't put it back after wrapping up the others for Mallory.

"Now that is a work of art." The man studied the cupcake as if it were the edible version of Michelangelo's *David*. "Are those pieces of Oreo?"

"They are."

"Amazing."

She smiled, gratified by his compliment, because it sounded so sincere. He seemed like one of those rare people who was truly fascinated by life, always stopping to study or stare, marvelling at the mechanics of something simple. It was a gift, to look at life like that, and one Olivia didn't think she had, although she was happy enough.

"So," she said after a few seconds when the man was simply staring at the cupcake, marvelling. "Are you, ah, going to buy it?"

"Buy it?" His eyebrows rose once more, with comical drama. "Of course I'm going to buy it! How much?"

"Two pounds fifty."

"You are grossly undercharging, then. Cupcakes the size of a small rodent go for nearly five pounds in London."

"What an unappealing comparison," Olivia returned with another laugh. "And this isn't London, it's the Cotswolds."

"So you should really be charging six pounds."

She laughed again, properly, and he grinned in return, and right then something in Olivia stirred to life, something that had been so dead and buried she'd forgotten it had even existed. But that tiny winkle of interest and yearning felt a bit like the poke of an electric cattle prod. *Whoa. I'm alive. Here is a man.*

And a man unlike any other she'd seen in Wychwood-on-Lea, which usually ran to golf-playing retirees and self-important City types, whose wives had dragged them out to experience so-called country living.

"Still, it's two pounds fifty," she said firmly. "I'm having a hard enough time selling them as it is."

"Are you? But you've only one left."

"I gave five away just now, and another one this morning." When Ellie had come in for a coffee and a chat. She grimaced good-naturedly as she confessed, "And I ate one myself."

"Which means you sold…?"

"Four."

"Think of the profit you could have made! Two pounds fifty extra per cupcake… That's…"

He frowned, and she supplied with a smile, "Ten pounds."

"Which is not to be sneezed at."

"No."

They smiled at each other, rather foolishly, or at least Olivia felt foolish. The banter had been witty and fun, but now that they had fallen silent, the man looked suddenly earnest and serious and she…she didn't know how she looked. Or felt.

"It must be hard running a tea shop in a village this size. Do you have much help?"

"No, it's just me." Which, for some ridiculous reason, nearly brought a wretched lump to her throat. How bizarre. "But it's fine," she said quickly. "It's all fine. You're right, though, Wychwood-on-Lea is a small place. Not as much foot traffic as I'd like, but I try to make up for it in other ways. Still, it's all good."

The man nodded slowly, in a way that made Olivia think he didn't believe her, which was exasperating because she was telling the truth. It was all good. Definitely.

"So the cupcake. Would you like it in a box?"

"You have boxes?" He sounded delighted, making Olivia smile again, and she went to fetch one of her many boxes.

"Tea on the Lea," he read off the front with satisfaction. "Very clever."

"Well, at least it rhymes. But I didn't come up with it. My mother did."

"Your mother?"

"It was her shop originally, but I took it over six months ago."

"So has this shop been in your family for ages? Should there be a sign over the door, 'Established in 1854' or something? 'Purveyors of Tea to the Queen'?"

She laughed and shook her head. "Sadly we have not supplied the Queen with anything. And my mum started the shop ten years ago, after she retired. It was always a dream of hers, to own a little shop like this."

"Kudos to her for following her dreams."

"Yes, exactly."

"And is it your dream as well?"

Goodness, this was getting rather personal. "It's become my dream," Olivia said firmly. "I love baking, and I'm happy here." Which, for some reason, made it sound as if she wasn't. As if she had to convince herself, which she didn't. "Anyway." Olivia took a length of silver ribbon she usually saved for her wedding cake orders and wrapped it around the box, tying it with an elegant bow. "There you are. That will be two pounds fifty."

"Why don't you charge me five pounds?" the man suggested as he handed over his debit card. "Really, I insist. It's practically a crime otherwise."

"Two pounds fifty," Olivia repeated firmly. "But if you come back again, I might have upped the prices by then."

"I certainly hope so. Do you make cupcakes every day?"

Olivia thought of Mallory's idea. "Actually, I'm running a promotion," she said a bit recklessly. "The Twelve Days of Cupcakes. A different flavour of cupcake every day in the run-up to Christmas…and if you buy one on each of the twelve days, you get a free one at the end. But you have to come every day." For some reason her heart had started beating fast as she said all this. She gazed at him, eyebrows raised. "What do you think?"

"That's an absolutely cracking idea. Simply cracking." He grinned. "Count me in."

Olivia's heart flipped over. She was being ridiculous, of course. She didn't even know this man and he was, it had to be said, a tiny bit on the eccentric side, with his enthusiastic manner, his endless scarf. But still. There went her heart. She reached for the card reader, unable to keep from glancing at the name on the debit card as she pushed it into the reader. Simon Blacklock. What a perfectly appropriate name—like something she'd read in an Austen or Brontë novel. Very Wuthering Heights-ish.

In some ways Simon Blacklock seemed like someone

from another century, with his friendly, open face, his interest in everything, even his battered tweed jacket and winding scarf. He was decidedly old-fashioned, and Olivia liked that about him.

"Put your PIN in please," she said, and pushed the reader towards him, averting her eyes while he pressed the numbers on the keypad.

He pushed it back towards her with a smile, and Olivia gave him his card back. She had a strange, almost panicky sense not to let him simply walk out the door, out of her life.

"Enjoy your cupcake," she blurted a little too fast. "And see you…again?" She cringed a little inwardly at how hopeful and eager she sounded.

"Yes, definitely." He hoisted the box. "I can't wait to try out some more flavours." And with one last whimsical smile, he was gone, the bells jingling as he shut the door behind him.

Chapter Two

OLIVIA PROWLED AROUND her flat later that evening, feeling unusually restless. She'd spent the rest of the afternoon finishing her shopping list and organising her storage area, hauling three boxes of Christmas decorations from the loft, without a single other person coming through the door.

At five o'clock she locked up the shop and headed upstairs to the flat she'd shared with her mum until two months ago, when Tina James had moved to a retired living housing development twenty minutes away in Witney. It still felt strange to be here alone, although Olivia had lived alone for fifteen years in London, in a shoebox-sized flat in Hackney.

Still, this place felt irrevocably her mum's; it was a poky little place, but not without its charm: two tiny bedrooms, a sitting room with views over the river and a tiny, cast-iron fireplace, a galley kitchen, and a bathroom that you could just about squeeze into. Olivia joked about being able to use the toilet, shower, and sink all at the same time, although she'd yet to accomplish that feat.

She and her mum had been constantly tripping over each other when they'd shared the small space, but it still seemed rather ridiculously big and empty without her there. After making a mug of instant noodles—hardly the most nutritious of suppers, but Olivia had never bothered with cooking for one—she collapsed onto the sofa, planning on an evening of Channel Four reality TV. Dr Jekyll, deciding to be friendly for once, leapt into her lap, making Olivia let out a startled *oof*. The cat really was enormous, and you never knew whether he was going to purr or unsheathe his claws, hence the name.

Olivia stroked him as she clicked the remote. Normally, after a day of work that had begun just before five a.m., she was grateful to sink into the sofa and watch some mindless telly. Tonight, for some reason, the prospect felt the teeniest, tiniest bit...well, *depressing*.

She needed to get a grip, Olivia told herself crossly. She was not the type of person to feel sorry for herself, not even for a moment, and in any case, there was nothing to feel sorry about. She had a job she loved, a nice home, a loving mum, plenty of friends, even this ridiculous cat. She didn't need anything. She was really quite sure of that.

She stroked Dr Jekyll again, a little too firmly this time, and with a resentful yowl he dug his claws in—*ouch*—and then lumbered off her lap, plopping onto the floor before stalking away, bushy tail raised high in dudgeon. Perhaps she wouldn't count the cat among her blessings quite yet, but still. She was happy; she was fulfilled. It was just everyone felt a little out of sorts, a bit restless, once in a while, didn't they? Of course they did.

The next morning Olivia was up bright and early to make her next batch of cupcakes. Last night, after turning off a trashy show about discontented and overly Botoxed housewives in some American city or other, she'd designed a banner for the shop window detailing the Twelve Days of Cupcakes, complete with a border of holly leaves and bright red berries, and pictures of various delicious cupcakes. She'd also made a card that customers could have stamped whenever they bought a cupcake; in a moment of determined optimism she'd printed a hundred of them. Her Art GCSE was being put to some small use, at least.

Now, in the inky darkness of pre-dawn, she reached for sacks of flour and sugar, a basket of eggs delivered fresh from a local farm three times a week. Even though her body ached with tiredness and her eyes felt gritty, she loved these moments in the little kitchen in the back of the tea shop, creating the concoctions that would fill the cake stand and display case that day. Baking was love; it was what her mother had done all her life, what she'd taught.

They hadn't had much when Olivia had been growing up; her father had walked out when she was two years old, never to come back, and Tina had held a variety of menial jobs to make ends meet. There hadn't been the money for extravagant holidays or new trainers or birthday parties, but there had always, *always* been cake—and biscuits and tarts and pies and meringues. Her mother splurged on sugar and flour, high-quality cooking chocolate and plenty of hundreds and thousands. And just about every day when Olivia had come home from school, there had been something delicious and still-warm on the kitchen table.

Tina had passed that love of baking on to Olivia; even when she'd been doing the nine-to-five (or really, eight-to-six) slog in London, she'd loved relaxing with a big bowl of butter and sugar to cream together. She'd always brought in tins of cakes and flapjacks, biscuits and tarts, to the office, happy for anyone to help themselves. And when a friend was down, a baby was born, anything to celebrate or mourn—well, baking always helped.

And it helped now, as the restlessness she'd felt last night morphed into cheerful purpose. She'd decided to try a new flavour of cupcake today—salted caramel, with a melting, caramel centre and a butterscotch sweet on top of the swirls of creamy icing. She'd pile them in the window, on her prized Victorian cake stand, with its intricate iron swirls to match the icing. With the banner, and a few boughs of holly and evergreen around, she thought it would look very Christmassy—and as it was only nineteen days until the twenty-fifth, certainly very timely.

While the cakes were cooling, Olivia ran upstairs to shower and change before opening the shop at half past seven, when she usually snagged a few customers grabbing a coffee and muffin on their way to work.

Sure enough, her friend Ava Tucker, recently married to Jace and with ten-month-old William in a pushchair, came in at quarter to eight to buy both items.

"I'm on the way to the childminder's," she explained while Olivia poured her coffee from the pot she always kept brewing. "I've got a big meeting in Oxford today—a partnership with an employment agency."

"Sounds very promising." A little over a year ago Ava had started her own business, training and equipping women to return to the workforce. As a not-for-profit, she helped women not only with obtaining the necessary computer and administrative skills, but also with the right clothes, confidence, and interview techniques.

"I hope so," she said as she reached down to wipe a bit of drool from William's adorably chubby chin. "It would be wonderful to make some more connections."

Olivia handed her the coffee and muffin, leaning over to give William a coo. He was adorable, with round red cheeks and a tuft of wheat-blond hair. Olivia had given up on having children herself a few years back when it looked as if there was no one in the offing—and there hadn't been—but she still loved a good cuddle. Fortunately, William was always available.

"I love the cupcake banner," Ava remarked as she broke off a piece of the muffin and handed it to William to gum.

"Twelve Days of Cupcakes! Very catchy."

"I hope so. It was Mallory's idea, actually."

"Was it? She's a clever one, isn't she? Too clever by half, I think."

"Yes, that's true," Olivia answered with a laugh. "She'll run rings around some poor bloke one day, I don't doubt."

"And Harriet and Richard as well." Ava glanced at her son with a smile. "Thankfully I've a few years to go before I have to worry about such things. I'll be applying for my OAP bus pass before William's dating."

"Not quite," Olivia said lightly. Ava was three years younger than she was.

"Almost," Ava answered with a grimace. "In any case, Jace would like a baby, as well." She looked away as she said it, making Olivia pause. She knew William was the son of Ava's first husband, who had died precipitously of a heart attack months before she met Jace.

"Is that something you want?" she asked carefully.

"I don't know. Babies are bloody hard work, you know?"

"I don't, but I can imagine."

"Oh sorry, Olivia, am I completely putting my foot in it?" Ava cried, aghast.

"Now you are," Olivia returned, smiling to take the sting out of the words. "Not everyone wants babies, Ava." She'd never been particularly maternal, but then she'd never given herself the chance to be, because it hadn't seemed like a possibility.

"Exactly. And I never thought I was the maternal type, to be honest. I love William to bits, but the thought of going through it all again…" She shuddered. "But it also seems so unfair to deny Jace the chance to be a father."

"He's a father to William."

"Yes, but his own… It does make a difference, don't you think?" She shook her head. "It shouldn't, I know, but I suppose it does."

"I don't know if it does or not," Olivia said slowly. "My father walked out when I was two years old. Biology didn't matter much there." She spoke matter-of-factly, without a hint of self-pity or sorrow. Her father's abandonment had been a part of her life for so long she didn't think it had the power to hurt her. Besides, Tina had more than made up for any deadbeat dad. She'd been—and still was—the most wonderful mum.

"Yes, too true," Ava answered on a sigh; Olivia knew she had a troubled family history. "Biology isn't everything, certainly."

William was starting to grizzle, and so Ava hoisted her coffee cup and gave Olivia a cheery wave. "I'd better get on. Are you coming to Harriet's on Friday for our girls' night in?"

"Yes, I'll be there. Wouldn't miss it for the world." Every month all five of them got together for a gossip and a drink, with much hilarity ensuing. Olivia had started to be included in these gatherings a little over a year ago, and she made sure never to miss a single one.

"Great, see you then," Ava chirped, and then she was out the door. From then until late morning Olivia had a steady trickle of customers, so she didn't get a chance to finish her window display until nearly lunchtime.

She nipped out back to the tiny garden behind the shop to cut some holly from the overgrown bush by the gate that led out to the river and the muddy footpath alongside it, and then she rustled up some red velvet ribbon, as well. On Sunday she'd do her big Christmas shop and get a few more bits and bobs to make the window display the best it could be.

The Twelve Days of Cupcakes. Outside, in the cold, crystalline air, she stepped back from the bow front of her shop to survey her work. Would people be tempted by the plate of gooey caramel cupcakes in the window? So far she hadn't sold one, but she had high hopes for this afternoon. If Mallory came in with her friends...

If Simon Blacklock came back...

He had, rather ridiculously, been at the back of her mind for most of the day. She'd gone over their few minutes of banterous chit-chat and decided she needed to stop remembering every single thing he'd said. He was a *stranger*, for heaven's sake, and he'd just been polite, in his own, charmingly eccentric way. The fact that he'd made her heart tumble right over was testament to the exceedingly single life she'd been living rather than any possible spark between them. She hadn't had a date in… No, she really didn't want to tot up the time. It had been years, at any rate. A lot of years.

With a sigh, Olivia headed back into the shop and its baking-scented warmth. This was her quietest part of the day, after her lunch rush (that was putting it rather optimistically) and before the brief pick-up in the late afternoon. Normally she used the time to crack on with a few jobs, but today that odd restlessness she'd felt last night came sneaking back.

Stupid to feel it. Stupid to let it matter. The shop was cosy and inviting, the cupcakes were pleasing to look at, and someone was warbling 'I'm dreaming of a white Christmas' on the radio. What was there to feel restless about?

Olivia turned up the volume on the radio and then reached for her laptop to start googling Christmas decoration ideas while keeping one eye on the front door.

At three o'clock Mallory breezed in with one of her best friends, Abby, who was Ellie's daughter.

Olivia had heard from Ellie a bit of the drama of their relationship; Mallory had been the cool girl to Abby's nerd but somehow between the small pond of primary school and the enormous ocean of the local comprehensive they'd found a little island of middle ground and were now practically inseparable, despite Mallory having a couple of friends (flicky-haired girls, she called them) that Abby couldn't stand.

"You did it!" Mallory cried as she burst through the door with so much energy that the glass pane rattled and Olivia winced.

"Yes, I did. What do you think?"

"It's fab. And those cupcakes look amazing. Can we have one each?"

"Of course," Olivia said. "It's the least I can do for the genius behind my inspiration."

"We'll pay for them," Mallory declared as Olivia took two cakes from the window and put them on doily-lined plates. "There's no point giving them away, is there?"

"You don't—"

"No, we will," Abby insisted.

"And then we'll be eligible for the free cake at the end!" Mallory crowed.

"Ah, now I see the method to your madness." The two girls sprawled at one of the tables while Olivia watched them affectionately. Twelve nearly thirteen—such a tricky age. She remembered it well herself; she'd been chubby, round-faced and freckly and fairly miserable, thanks to some mean girls in her year. Mallory had had a run-in with her own mean girls, and Olivia was glad she'd come out whole, if not completely unscathed.

Two more of Mallory's friends came in a short while later, and to Olivia's gratification they each bought a cupcake. Then a moody-looking sixth form boy with super-gelled hair and a sulky expression strode in, causing Mallory and her friends to look up and nudge each other. He bought two cupcakes, and a little while later a mum bought four for her family's pudding that night. It seemed people were taking notice of her sign, not to mention the offer of a free cupcake at the end. Olivia had stamped their cards with cheerful enthusiasm. Perhaps this idea really would take off.

She'd already sold ten cupcakes, and there were only two left. It was half past four and the shop had emptied out, and Olivia hoped that one of the cupcakes had a certain person's name on it. *Simon Blacklock*. Was she mad, thinking this way—or just pathetic? Wishful, at the very least.

The clock ticked slowly to the hour and no one came in. It was dark outside now; people were hurrying home, heads tucked low against the bitter December wind. Olivia tidied up and then toyed with designs for a customer loyalty card on a notepad, looking up to check the door every few minutes, only to catch sight of her own rather woebegone reflection in the darkened pane. Maybe he wasn't coming. That really shouldn't disappoint her as much as it clearly did.

It wasn't even him, Olivia thought even though she knew it sort of was. But it was also the fact that something so small, so seemingly inconsequential, could become so important to her. A couple minutes, if that, of chit-chat, and here she was, glancing hopefully towards the door yet again.

Another hour passed by with agonising slowness, and yet all too fast. Olivia sorted through her boxes of Christmas decorations, binning the dodgy lights with their too-tangled cords and dusting off the porcelain nativity set she placed on the Victorian stand in the centre of the shop. Already things were starting to look a bit more Christmassy, and it gave her a little lift, even as she fought a growing disappointment as time ticked relentlessly on.

Finally, at quarter past five, Olivia flipped the sign to closed—something she usually did at five—and rather disconsolately started wiping tables and stacking chairs.

Don't be disappointed, she told herself. *Don't be a complete ninny.* And maybe get out more, besides the wine nights at Willoughby Close. Maybe she'd join one of those wretched dating sites. Oh, no. She wasn't ready for that. But something else, perhaps… The village had loads of clubs. Bridge, crocheting, cricket. Admittedly most of the clubs attracted either OAPs or children, but perhaps she could find something suited to someone like her—middle-aged and single.

The shop tidied, she glanced at two cupcakes in all of their salted caramel glory, the glossy buttercream piled on top of the spongy cake in lovely swirls.

"Oh, screw it, then," she said on a sigh, and taking one of the cupcakes, she peeled the paper away from the cake and took a big, gooey bite.

A tapping on the door had Olivia turning far too fast, her mouth still full of caramel and cake. And then her heart was turning, over and over, as she caught sight of the familiar—well, somewhat—figure standing in the window, scarf wrapped around his neck, eyebrows raised in a hopeful way.

Swallowing so fast she nearly choked, her mouth still full of sweetness, she walked quickly to the door and flipped the lock, unable to keep from grinning even though she suspected she had icing on her teeth.

"Am I too late?" Simon asked in a dramatically aggrieved way as she opened the door and stepped aside so he could come in. She was still smiling.

"Almost."

"Are there any cupcakes left?" He nodded towards the window. "The cake stand…"

"Is empty. I've kept one behind for you, just in case." She blushed, wondering if that was too…well, *something*.

"You are amazing! A saint and a wonder." He grinned. "Am I laying it on too thick?"

"Perhaps," Olivia acknowledged with a little laugh, although truth be told she liked his rather theatrical manner.

"Here you are." She fetched the last cupcake and presented it to him with a flourish. Simon took it, a slightly odd, whimsical look on his face as he gazed at her.

"What…" Olivia said, starting to blush all over again.

"You've a bit of icing on your mouth…"

"Oh." Now she was turning a lovely—or not—shade of scarlet as she managed an unsteady laugh. "Whoops…" She rubbed her mouth a bit frantically, but Simon shook his head and then, leaning forward, he touched the corner of her mouth with his thumb. It was a brief yet tantalising gesture, and it felt shockingly intimate. It made Olivia realise just how long it had been since she'd been touched, in any way, by a man. Too long.

"Sorry." Now he was the one who was blushing, a faint rosy tint to his lean cheeks as he stepped back. "I didn't…"

"It's okay." She turned away quickly, trying to hide how unsettled that little touch had made her. How it made her mind jump to other, more extensive possibilities. What was *wrong* with her? "Would you like a box?" she asked, speaking so fast that her words jumbled into one another. "And a ribbon?"

"Um, yes, sure." Simon sounded as unsettled as she was, which was both faintly gratifying and…more unsettling. This was getting too weird.

Olivia felt as if she were all thumbs as she fetched a box from the pantry, jamming the sides and flaps together, her mind a blur. *Quick, think of something to say…something innocuous and witty…*

"Did you like yesterday's cupcake?" she asked a bit desperately. "The cookies and cream."

"Ah, well." Simon looked a bit embarrassed, his smile apologetic. "It looked absolutely delicious, of course, but I didn't eat it."

"You didn't?"

In an icy flash of horror, Olivia pictured him giving the cupcake to someone else—his adorable girlfriend, his pregnant wife, his little daughter. *Of course* he had people like that in his life.

"No, I gave it to…to someone else. But they enjoyed it, I assure you."

Which left Olivia feeling even more awkward, because there was no way she could ask him to whom he'd given his cupcake, and he seemed almost reluctant to impart the information.

"Well, I hope you enjoy this one," she said, every word stilted. "Salted caramel. That is, if you're the one eating it."

Simon just smiled, which made her feel worse. What was he not saying, and why? Or was she reading way too much into what was essentially a business exchange? She handed him the box. "Here you are."

"Thank you so much. And here you are." He handed her a five-pound note, his fingers brushing hers. "And no change. I absolutely insist."

Which just felt like pity now. "Thank you," Olivia said. "And…see you tomorrow?"

"I'll be here." He smiled, gave a mock salute, and then, far too soon, he was gone, the door banging shut behind him, letting in a gust of icy air that made Olivia shiver as she stared disconsolately out at the darkness.

Chapter Three

"COME IN, COME in!"

Harriet urged Olivia inside, brandishing a very full glass of white wine as her adorable dog Daisy frolicked about their heels, nearly making them both trip.

"Thanks." Olivia smiled as she stepped across the threshold of Harriet's converted-stable cottage at Willoughby Close. Ava, Ellie, and Alice were already inside, sprawled across the matching sofas. "Where's Richard?"

"Upstairs, corralling the children. I've told them they will come down on pain of death, or at least a serious scolding, even Richard." She plucked the bottle of average plonk Olivia had been holding. "You shouldn't have, but I'm glad you did. I ruined the mulled wine with far too much orange juice, and we're already mostly through the bottle of white Ava brought."

"Oh, really?" Everyone's glasses looked very full, Olivia noticed, and wondered what they were celebrating—or bemoaning.

"Let me get you a glass," Alice offered as she rose from

the sofa. "There's still some white left…"

"Or this red." Harriet placed Olivia's bottle on the kitchen counter with a thunk. "What do you fancy?"

"Either is fine," Olivia answered with a smile as she unbuttoned her parka. It was good to be with her friends, especially on a wet and windy winter's night, where the only company she would have had was Dr Jekyll, who was definitely in full Mr Hyde mode at the moment.

"I'll let you finish off the white, then," Alice said cheerfully, and poured Olivia a glass to the brim before handing it over with a smile.

"So how is everyone?" Olivia asked as she plopped herself down in the middle of one of the sofas, between Ava and Ellie. Harriet flung herself onto the other one with a sigh, and Alice curled up in the opposite corner.

"We're fine," Ellie began, only to have her face crumple a little bit. Olivia sat up in alarm, sloshing her wine over her hand.

"Ellie…?"

"Oh, it's nothing, really," Ellie said as she fished for a hanky and blew her nose. "I'm being hormonal and weepy for no good reason."

"That's not true," Ava fired back. "It's a big deal, Ellie."

"What is?" Olivia asked. She felt as if she'd missed part of a crucial conversation.

Ellie took a shuddering breath and a gulp of wine. "Oliver and I—and Abby, of course—are moving to Oxford in

January."

"What!" Olivia stared at her in surprise and dismay. "But...why?"

"We both work in Oxford, and it makes sense to be closer," Ellie said, sounding rather resigned. "And Abby's been accepted for the next term to Headington Girls."

"She's going to a *girls'* school?"

"She wants to," Ellie said. "She pushed the application."

"But..." Olivia was at a loss, although she realised she didn't know Abby all that well. Mallory did most of the talking.

"She's very driven," Ellie said. "Unlike me. And a lot of the students at the comp mess about. It's a good school, but she has the drive and Oliver has the money, so..." She shrugged. "Besides, it wasn't really working, both of us commuting."

"Right." Olivia's mind whirled. She'd come to depend on this little group of five. She hated the thought of losing even one of her dear friends.

"Well, you're not the only one who is thinking of a move," Harriet said with a wry smile. "Richard and I put an offer on a house on the other side of the village, and it's been accepted. All things being equal, we should be able to move out by March."

"What...!"

"You did?"

"Where?"

Harriet waved away all their surprised questions with a smile. "On the rougher side, as it were…an old wreck, but it's what we could afford, and the truth is, we're squeezed in this little place."

"I can't believe it," Ava cried. "Willoughby Close will be completely empty." Alice had moved into Willoughby Manor last year, when she'd married Henry Trent, and Ava had moved into the caretaker's cottage with Jace. Their cottages hadn't been let yet, and now the other two would be vacated, as well. It was strange to think of the cheerful little courtyard with its cluster of four cottages completely unoccupied. Olivia didn't like it.

"Everyone's moving on in one way or another, aren't they?" Alice said with a nostalgic sigh. "It makes me feel a little sad, somehow."

It made Olivia feel sad, as well. Everyone was moving on in some way…but her. She sat back and sipped her wine as the conversation swirled around her, talk of jobs and houses, babies and children. All her friends were married; all of them had children save for Alice, who had a manor and a charity to run, and was likely to start a family in the near future. All of them, Olivia acknowledged with a funny little pang she wasn't used to feeling, had lives that suddenly seemed far fuller and busier than her own.

She'd never minded it before, or at least, she acknowledged, she hadn't *let* herself mind. She didn't need a partner or family to feel fulfilled and connected to her community.

She *knew* that, and yet at the moment she felt like an appendage rather than an integral part. It wasn't the best feeling.

"Well, we're not going anywhere," Ava said as she settled back into the sofa. "Jace is happy at the manor...and I'm happy too." Her smile was a tiny bit brittle, reminding Olivia that Ava wasn't ready to have another baby and Jace seemed as if he was. No one's life was perfect, including her own.

"What about you, Olivia?" Ellie asked. "Anything new and exciting happening at Tea on the Lea?"

For some ridiculous reason Olivia thought of Simon Blacklock. He'd come in for his cupcake yesterday at a quarter to five, just when she'd started to worry that he wouldn't. Her heart had done that silly tumble in her chest and she'd acted as if she hadn't been saving a pistachio and strawberry cupcake just for him, having kept one back after selling the other eleven. The cupcake promotion was really working; people seemed interested in the loyalty cards, and the window display as well as word of mouth drew them in.

When Simon had bought his cupcake, they'd barely spoken, which had disappointed her more than it should have; he'd been his usual charming self, but clearly distracted and in a rush, and considering how she'd been looking forward to seeing him all day—again, ridiculous—the two-minute exchange had ended up making her feel rather flat.

"Nothing, really," she said now, and Harriet, ever

shrewd, arched an eyebrow.

"It took you long enough to reply. What were you thinking about telling us?"

Olivia's cheeks started to warm. "Nnn…nothing," she stammered, and Harriet folded her arms and stared her down.

"Nothing? You're *blushing*."

"And stammering," Ellie contributed helpfully, looking interested. "What's going on, Olivia?"

Perhaps it was because all her friends seemed to have busier lives, or maybe it was just the glass of wine she'd bolted down without much dinner beforehand, but for some contrary reason Olivia felt reckless, something she usually didn't feel. She'd always lived her life in a steady, measured way, but in that moment she wanted to share something exciting, to *have* something exciting to share.

"Oh, it really is nothing," she said with a little laugh, or at least an attempt at one. "A bloke has come into the shop every day since I started my cupcake promotion." Everyone stared at her, waiting for more, and suddenly Olivia didn't feel reckless anymore, just a bit pathetic. "That's it," she finished a little flatly, and then drained the last of her wine.

"That can't be it," Ava said after a moment. "Or you wouldn't have mentioned it. What is this bloke like?"

Olivia shrugged, hating having everyone's eyes on her. She was never the centre of attention; all her life she'd played a supporting role, and she'd liked that…until now, it seemed. Honorary auntie, BFF with the wine and the tissues after someone else's breakup, concerned colleague, friendly baker, kindly neighbour. She was happy in those roles; she felt comfortable in them. They were safe. Now the spotlight had swung on her and she squirmed. A lot.

"Does he buy a cupcake?" Ellie asked with a kindly smile, clearly trying to help her out. Olivia smiled back, a bit tightly. Her friends were lovely, and they were trying so hard, but when everyone else was talking about husbands and houses and babies, a stranger buying a cupcake in her shop just felt...sad. It wasn't exciting. It wasn't *news*.

"Yes, he does," she finally said on a sigh.

"The important question is, is he fit?" Ava asked, her eyes narrowing in assessment. "He must be, or you wouldn't have mentioned him."

Fit? Olivia doubted Ava would think Simon Blacklock was *fit*. She was married to Jace, who oozed sex appeal and magnetic charisma from every pore. As for Simon...Olivia pictured his rangy figure, his slightly too-long hair, his colourful scarf, his glinting grey-green eyes.

"He's...interesting," she said at last. This was met with a chorus of enthusiastic oohs.

"And he must be interested in you," Ellie said excitedly, "to buy a cupcake every single day."

"It's just because I'm running this promotion—"

"What man buys a cupcake three days running?" Harriet demanded.

"I don't think he eats them himself," Olivia interjected. "He said as much, really."

"Then who does he give them to?"

"Maybe his poor, widowed mother?" Ellie suggested helpfully.

"Or a homeless person?" Alice added.

"There aren't any homeless people in Wychwood-on-Lea," Harriet protested, and then fell silent, looking slightly abashed. Alice had been homeless before she'd landed a job taking care of Lady Stokeley, her husband's great-aunt, until she'd died a year ago.

"Maybe he buys them for his girlfriend or his wife," Olivia broke into their happily-ever-after musings. "Or his adorable little child. Honestly, everyone. It isn't like that."

"But it must be a little like that," Ellie persisted, "for you to have mentioned it at all."

"I shouldn't have—"

"There must have been a little bit of flirting," Ava added shrewdly. "A little banter over the buttercream? Cosying up with the cupcakes?"

"Oh, honestly." Laughing, Olivia tossed a throw pillow at her, and Ava caught it, smiling. "Maybe a tiny bit," she allowed, and was subjected to another chorus of excited squeals. "But nothing much."

"Do you know his name?"

For some reason Olivia didn't want to reveal Simon's name. He hadn't actually introduced himself, after all. It felt a little stalkerish, to say his name when she'd got it from his debit card. "No."

"Well, that's your goal for tomorrow," Harriet announced. "Learn Mystery Man's name."

"I'll try." Saturdays were a bit hit or miss; sometimes she got a boatload of walkers and day-trippers, other times the shop stayed empty all day. As for Simon Blacklock? Would he show up on a Saturday? Did he even live in Wychwood? She realised how little she knew about him; in fact she knew *nothing* about him except perhaps that he was a bit clumsy.

"What's everyone doing for Christmas?" Olivia asked in a blatant bid to shift the attention from herself. "Will you all be in Willoughby Close?"

Thankfully the conversation moved on; Harriet was going to her parents for Christmas, and Alice and Henry would be at the manor, with at least a dozen guests coming from London. Ellie was heading up north, and Ava and Jace were having their first Christmas with baby William.

"What about you, Olivia? Would you like to come to ours?" Alice asked.

Olivia shook her head. Christmas at Willoughby Manor would be lovely, with roaring fires and a table for twenty groaning with food, but she already had plans. "I'll be in Witney, with Mum." She always had Christmas with her mum—a present each in the morning, a roast dinner for two, and a glass of sherry while listening to the Queen's speech.

"How is your mum getting on in her new flat?" Ava asked.

"Okay, I think." Olivia visited her mother every Sunday afternoon, and so far Tina had seemed to like it well enough, but sometimes she worried that her mother's retirement at age seventy-three had doused some spark inside her. "I'm hoping she gets more involved with all the things they have on. It's quite a community—there's bridge, tennis, even salsa dancing."

"I can see Tina enjoying that," Harriet said, and Olivia smiled. A few years ago, perhaps, she could have seen her mum throwing herself into those sorts of things, but she lived a much quieter life now—just as Olivia did.

By the time she left Willoughby Close, feeling slightly tiddly after two glasses of wine, Olivia's good humour was mostly restored. Her friends were wonderful, and so what if they had husbands and houses and all the rest? Olivia had always maintained that if she'd really wanted to get married, she would have done.

She'd had a few boyfriends over the years, but no one she'd felt like going the distance with, and if marriage and babies had been that important to her, she suspected she would have put a ring on it regardless.

As it was, she'd always liked her own company, as well as her freedom, although running Tea on the Lea had kept her in one place, precluding holidays, for the last few years. She'd told herself that once she got the shop on steady financial footing, she'd close it for a week and go away somewhere tropical and relaxing, but she hadn't managed that yet.

Olivia breathed in the frosty night air as she turned down the road towards Wychwood's high street. The sky was full of stars, the air clear and cold. A huge Christmas tree had been erected in the middle of the village green, now a dark, hulking shape under the moonlight; the official turning on of its lights would be on Wednesday, and Olivia was planning to keep the shop open, with some extra Christmas goodies available, and invitations for her mince pies and mulled wine evening the following week to be handed out.

As she turned down the high street, she noticed the Christmas lights that had been strung between the ancient buildings, and the star of Bethlehem on top of the parish church, all waiting for the official ceremony on Wednesday.

Everything felt expectant and hushed, just as it must have been two thousand years ago. Olivia smiled at the thought, the last of her restlessness banished.

She had a good life here, even if it wasn't the same kind of busy as her friends'. Still smiling, she unlocked the door to the shop and headed to the stairs in the back, her cosy flat, and the ever-changing affections of Dr Jekyll.

"OH, OLIVIA, YOU shouldn't have."

Tina James took the scarlet poinsettia Olivia presented with a pleased smile and a slightly fretful air. "I wasn't thinking to decorate all that much really, but a plant is always nice."

"Not decorate!" Olivia planted her hands on her hips in not-so-mock outrage as she glanced around the compact open-plan living area of her mother's retirement flat. It was Sunday afternoon, and she'd spent a rainy, rather miserable Saturday on her own in the shop, unpacking Christmas decorations and stringing lights and ribbons in an attempt to stave off any flicker of loneliness. No one came in all day, so she might as well have closed the shop and spent the day doing errands or even just reading a book.

She'd flipped the sign to closed firmly at five, refusing to wait for Simon Blacklock to make an appearance. The twelve triple chocolate cupcakes she'd baked she'd brought here to donate to the communal lounge, and she'd told herself not to mope about it. She'd sold all her cupcakes on Friday, and none on Saturday. That was simply the nature of the business. Perhaps she wouldn't bother making cupcakes next Saturday, and make the cupcake promotion Monday to Friday only. "Why not, Mum?" she asked now. "You've always loved decorating."

Even when they'd been living in a poky little flat in Middlesbrough, her mother had made sure to garland it with holly and evergreen. There had always been a real, live Christmas tree adorned with glittering baubles, and oranges studded with cloves nestling in a bowl, filling the small space with festive fragrance. Olivia had spent hours playing with the ceramic figures of a well-worn and well-loved nativity set.

"Oh, but there isn't much point here, is there, really?" Tina said with a shrug. "Cup of tea?"

"Yes, please." Olivia placed the tin of shortbread she'd brought for her mum on the kitchen table, a feeling of unease rippling through her. She'd had her doubts about her mother moving to the sensible but seemingly soulless flat in nearby Witney; her mum had loved the cosy little flat above the shop, as well as paying attention to all the village comings and goings. Admittedly there had been more goings than comings, at least into the shop, but still. Tina had felt a part of things. She didn't know a soul in Witney.

"Have you gone to one of those bridge mornings?" Olivia asked brightly as Tina filled the kettle at the sink. "You always talk about trying one out."

Tina shook her head, her back to Olivia. "I don't think I'll go. I'm getting too old for cards."

"Too old… Mum, you're only seventy-three." Olivia gazed at her mother in uneasy alarm. She'd read about how retiring and moving to communities that catered for elderly residents could age a person, make them feel isolated and old before their time. She just never imagined her mother would feel that way.

"Still." Tina shrugged. "Bridge is such a fussy game, anyway."

"But you love bridge." Tina had taught her the game when she was still in primary school, complicated as it was.

She'd deal out all four hands on the kitchen table and they'd play two each while Tina talked her through all the complex bidding rules.

"I used to." Tina gave her a rueful smile. "Things change. Anyway, tell me, how things are at Tea on the Lea?"

"They're fine. I've brought you some shortbread. I'm running a cupcake promotion before Christmas."

"Cupcakes…!"

"Yes, one per day," Olivia said, and then proceeded to explain all about the promotion, never mind that she hadn't sold any yesterday. Her mother listened avidly, but after a few minutes Olivia could tell her mind was elsewhere, and she tried not to feel worried, or worse, hurt. Her mother was usually eager for all the details, wanted to know about the shop she'd started ten years ago.

"What can I do to help?" she asked once they'd finished their tea. "Any errands need running? Ironing? How about a good scrub out of the toilet?"

"Oh, Olivia, I'm not an invalid." To Olivia's surprise her mother almost sounded annoyed. "I'm perfectly capable of doing those things myself."

"Of course you are," she answered after a moment, trying to sound cheerful rather than offended. "I'm just trying to help, Mum."

"Oh, darling, I know." Tina sighed and then reached across the table to squeeze Olivia's hand. "Please forgive my grumpiness. I'm feeling a bit out of sorts, and I don't even know why."

"Is it because it's Christmas?" Olivia asked gently. "You always did up the flat so nicely…"

"I don't know what it is. Just getting used to being here, I suppose."

"We could have Christmas at the flat over the shop instead of here," Olivia suggested. "I haven't got a tree yet, but I was planning on it…"

"A tree in that flat? It would take up half the sitting room."

"A tabletop one, then. Like you did last year." Her mum had had a small tree in the flat for ten years; it didn't make sense for her to resist now. Still, Tina just shook her head. "They do a nice lunch here on Christmas Day. I think I'll just go to that."

"What?" Olivia stared at her mother, startled and dismayed. "But I thought we'd be spending the day together, the way we always do?"

"We can, of course, but I'm sure you have better things to do, haven't you?" Olivia blinked, trying not to feel hurt. She'd spent Christmas Day with her mother every single year of her life. Why on earth was her mum backing out now? She almost sounded as if she didn't *want* Olivia there.

"I don't have better things to do, Mum," she said after a moment. "Of course I don't. Why don't you come to the flat? Or we could go to Alice and Henry's… You remember my friends?" Tina gave a little shake of her head, and Olivia couldn't tell if she didn't remember or didn't want to go. "They've invited us to Willoughby Manor for Christmas dinner." Although she'd already turned down Alice's invitation, Olivia knew it would always be open. "It's lovely…a big manor in the countryside, roaring fires…"

"Oh, I don't know." Tina rose from the table, the teacups rattling in their saucers as she whisked them to the sink. "I'll think about it, I suppose."

"Do. Even if we don't go there, we could still spend the day together."

"Yes, well, we'll see." Tina's tone was repressive, and so Olivia dropped the subject, still feeling uneasy.

Soon after that she couldn't think of any reason to stay longer, and as her mum seemed restless, almost wanting her to go, she decided to take her leave even though she'd only been there a little over an hour.

"I suppose I should get going," she said as she reached for her coat. "I still have my weekly shop to do." Tina stood by the sink, her arms folded, her smile a little distant. "You are…you are happy here, Mum?" Olivia couldn't keep from asking, needing the reassurance. "Aren't you?"

Tina looked surprised, and then, to Olivia's dismay, her gaze slid away from hers. "Yes," she said. "Of course I am. Don't worry about me, Olivia."

But of course she did worry, unable to keep from going over their conversation as she stocked up at Waitrose, adding some Christmas decorations—a porcelain angel, another set of fairy lights—to top up her supply. She bought her baking supplies in bulk from a wholesaler and had them delivered, but she enjoyed browsing the baking aisle and getting a few extras—edible gold stars, a tube of silver icing.

Back in Wychwood-on-Lea, Olivia tried to banish her worries and hurt by finishing the decoration of the shop. So far she had strung fairy lights all around, and lined the display cases and stands with red velvet ribbon. A sprig of mistletoe adorned the front door, whose brass handle now sported a cluster of jingle bells. She'd cut fresh holly and placed it in the corners of the display case, and now she added the newly purchased angel to the display case, and strung some more lights outside, to make the shop a bit more welcoming as dusk began earlier and earlier.

As the sun started to sink, the high street lost in shadow, she decided to start on a batch of mince pies for the Christmas light turn-on on Wednesday. It was time for Christmas baking, cupcakes included, to begin in earnest.

Baking always helped to banish worry; the methodical mixing, rolling out of dough, cutting the shapes helped to give her a focus and soothe her spirit. It reminded her of her childhood, standing next to her mum on top of a little stool, tiny hands patting out the dough or stirring the batter as her mother lovingly instructed her.

Soon, with the little kitchen in the back of the shop full of delicious, spicy smells, and Christmas carols blasting from the battered CD player in the corner, Olivia started to feel better. Her mum was probably just feeling a bit unsettled, being in a new place for Christmas.

And now that she had a little space to sort through her own thoughts, Olivia remembered that her mother protested them spending Christmas together just about every year, worried that Olivia was giving up more exciting plans to be with her mum. Maybe her protests this year hadn't been quite as half-hearted as they had been in the past, but still. There was nothing to worry about, surely. Her mum was in a period of adjustment, just as she was. They'd both get over it soon, Olivia reassured herself. Of course they would.

She had just slid the first tray of mince pies out of the oven, admiring their perfectly baked tops, puffed and golden, when a determined tapping on the front door had her straightening in surprise. The shop was clearly closed, even though the lights were on. It was after five on a dark and wintry Sunday evening.

Still the tapping continued, and Olivia went to see who couldn't read a closed sign.

She nearly stumbled in her step as she saw the tall, rangy figure by the door, his nose nearly pressed to the glass.

Fumbling with the lock, her heart doing its silly dance once more, Olivia opened the door.

"Sorry, am I too late? Are you closed?" Simon asked as he pushed an unruly lock of dark hair away from his forehead.

"I am closed," Olivia admitted even though she half didn't want to. "I was just baking mince pies for tomorrow."

"Mince pies…" There was a note of longing in his voice that made her smile.

"Would you like to come in and have one?" Olivia asked, feeling bold, and the smile that bloomed across Simon's face was answer enough.

"I'd love to," he said, and stepped inside.

Chapter Four

OLIVIA BUSIED HERSELF with fetching two mince pies from the back, all the while giving herself a stern talking-to to calm down. She arranged the pies on plates decorated with lace doilies, and then scrapped the doilies as a step too far, even though she normally served them with everything.

"Here we are," she called out cheerfully, bringing the plates to one of the tables at the front of the shop, only to stop uncertainly at the apologetic look on Simon's face.

"I'm so sorry...but I can't stay."

"Oh." Olivia willed herself not to blush as she glanced down at the two plates, her expectation so cringingly obvious. Thank heaven she hadn't used the doilies.

"I should have said," Simon continued. "I'm an absolute oaf—but you know that already, don't you? From when I nearly knocked your Victoria sponge over—"

"And the lemon drizzle." Olivia did her best to sound wry as she fetched a paper napkin and wrapped the mince pie up in it before thrusting it towards him "Here you are, then.

Enjoy."

"How much…?"

She waved him away, half wanting him gone. Actually, *all* wanting him gone. She felt so stupid, so obvious, hoping that he'd sit down with her and have a chat. Clearly he just wanted her baked goods. "It's on the house."

"No—"

"Really." Her voice came out sounding the tiniest bit hard, and she tried to soften it with a smile.

He stared at her for a moment, his paper-wrapped pie in his hand, a look of regret on his face, etched deep into the lines running from his nose to his mouth. "The reason I have to run off," he said at last, "is because I'm playing in an Advent carol concert at the parish church in half an hour. You…you don't fancy coming, do you?"

"Coming…" Olivia repeated blankly, too shocked to process what he was saying, and now Simon was the one who was blushing.

"Sorry, I should have introduced myself first, shouldn't I?" He stuck out a hand. "Simon Blacklock."

"Olivia James." She took his hand, his fingers tightening on hers, his palm warm and dry. She noticed he had calluses on the fingers of his left hand, and she wondered what instrument he played.

"So." Simon withdrew his hand, smiling. "Concert. Starting at six, if you fancy it. Mince pies and mulled wine after, but I'm sure yours are better." His smile was wry, a bit apologetic, almost as if he were bracing himself for a polite refusal.

And Olivia almost did refuse…although she wasn't even sure why she would. After all, why shouldn't she go to the concert? Staying home alone all evening was the only other option, and she'd had enough of that, really.

"All right, then," she said, seeming to surprise them both. "I'd love to come. But I should probably change…"

"Oh, it's casual, don't worry," Simon said hurriedly. "I'd better be off now—but I'll see you there? And after?"

After. He almost made it sound like a quasi-date, even though Olivia knew he was just talking about the standard mulled-wine-and-mince-pies that accompanied just about every public gathering this time of year, including her own.

"Yes," she said firmly. "And after."

With one last fleeting smile of farewell, Simon headed out into the dark night and after locking the door and putting the mince pies away, Olivia scurried upstairs to get herself concert-ready.

Obviously she couldn't look as if she were trying too hard since Simon had told her it was casual and it most certainly wasn't a date, but Olivia knew she needed to do better than her old jeans, a jumper dusted with flour, and her hair in a complete frizz.

Quickly she squeezed herself into a pair of skinny jeans—although there was nothing very skinny about her in them—and a forgiving tunic-style cashmere jumper in a

Christmassy green that brought out the barest glint of hazel in her mud-brown eyes. Some expensive hair products that she defiantly splurged on took care of most of the frizz, although, thanks to having been busy in a hot kitchen for the better part of an hour, her hairstyle did not resemble the gentle waves her various potions and products promised.

Dr Jekyll came into her tiny bedroom and wound between her legs, his bottle-brush tail waving high as he meowed plaintively.

"Dinner. Right." She gave him a stroke but he ducked away, hissing, showing his Hyde-like nature as he often did. Olivia's stomach growled in sympathy—she hadn't eaten anything since mid-morning—but she didn't have time to eat before the concert.

As it was, she hurried to open a tin of cat food for Dr Jekyll, and then grabbed her coat, giving her reflection one last hard stare, before heading out into the darkened night.

Quite a few people were heading towards the church at the bottom of the high street. Olivia was slightly ashamed to realise she'd only been there a few times since she'd moved to the village, for her friends' weddings.

Her mum had taken her to church when she'd been little, but she'd fallen out of the habit when she'd moved to London and Sundays mornings had been for lie-ins. Now nostalgia enveloped her in its misty memory as she stepped through the ancient wooden doors and into the candlelit interior; the dusty, musty smell of old hymnals and candle wax took her right back to her childhood.

Someone at the door handed her a program, and she took it with murmured thanks, scanning the pews for Simon but not seeing him anywhere. Since he was one of the musicians she wasn't surprised, but she still felt the tiniest bit disappointed.

She slid into a pew midway down the church and settled back, enjoying the sense of serenity that pervaded the soaring space. Creamy candles garlanded with holly adorned the end of each pew, as well as the choir stalls at the front. A small orchestra had been set up at the front of the church, and curiosity sparked inside her as she wondered again what instrument Simon played. She really didn't know anything about him, and she hoped she'd have the opportunity to learn more tonight.

The church soon filled up and a few minutes later the vicar, a kindly looking man in his fifties, introduced the service. A few seconds after that the musicians came out, and Olivia recognised Simon's rangy form instantly. He took his seat behind a cello, and she decided that seemed exactly right for him. The cello, the instrument closest to the human voice, the sound beautiful, emotional, a little melancholy.

She watched, unable to tear her gaze away, as he picked up his bow, his head bent over the cello, almost as if in prayer. Then the music started, filling the space, soaring up to the ceiling high above. *O Come, O Come, Emmanuel...*

The congregation rose to sing, as the music continued to

wend its way through the space. Olivia couldn't remember the last time she'd heard live music, and each note plucked at her soul now, the sonorous melody, the beautiful words, the sense of expectation, for all the songs, being Advent hymns and carols, were about waiting. *Rejoice... for something good is coming... something you can't even imagine...*

As the congregation sat down for an orchestral piece, Olivia found her gaze sneaking to Simon again, his long fingers gripping the cello and bow, an unruly lock of hair sliding forward, obscuring his face. He wore a crisp blue button-down shirt with the sleeves rolled up to his forearms and a pair of brown cords, and Olivia's heart gave a little lurch as she watched him play.

I like him, she realised with a jolt. Not just a fun crush or a passing interest, the way she'd panned it off to her friends. She thought of the way his eyes lit up, the easy, goofy smile, the enthusiasm about everything that he seemed to have. *I really like him and I want to get to know him better.*

It had been a long time since she'd felt that way about anyone, the interest along with the hope. A long time since she'd even considered putting herself out there, risking her pride along with her comfort to meet and reach another person.

She would be forty next birthday, after all, and she was rather set in her ways. Relationships at her age were a whole other kettle of fish than when you were in your twenties or even thirties, when you hadn't become settled in your life, the crow's feet making their faint prints on your skin, as well as the scars into your soul. When you'd fought for happiness and found it, and inviting someone new in meant risking overturning everything.

Of course, she was getting way ahead of herself now. She barely knew Simon, and his invitation for her to come to this concert might have been no more than the actions of a keen musician, a kindly neighbour, or both. She would be foolish to read anything more into it, and yet…

And yet, *she* felt something more, and that was enough to make her want to act. Take a risk, even if it was just asking Simon out for a drink. Olivia imagined telling her friends what she'd got up to at their next wine evening and she smiled at the thought.

When the evening had ended, the musicians all took a quick bow before filing out, leaving Olivia to mill around in the back of the church with the other concert-goers, sipping a plastic cup of mulled wine and nibbling a mince pie that definitely was not as good as hers.

She saw a few people she knew, and chatted to Gwyneth Larsen, the dear old lady who bought a box of macaroons from her several times a week. A school mum who had come in several times for coffee wished her a happy Christmas, and Edith Payne, a friend of her mother's who had afternoon tea twice a week like clockwork, buttonholed her by the drinks table.

"How is Tina, Olivia?" she asked with beady-eyed concern. "I keep meaning to visit her in Witney but they've stopped the bus service there and I don't drive…"

"I'll take you," Olivia offered. "I visit her every Sunday."

"Oh, that would be lovely, dear. I do miss her."

"I'm sure she'd love to see you." Perhaps visiting with an old friend would cheer her mum up. Even though Olivia had decided she was overreacting about her mum's state, she was still worried. Tina definitely hadn't seemed like herself that afternoon.

"And how are you getting on?" Edith asked, giving Olivia's elbow a sympathetic squeeze. "Managing that shop all on your own?"

"It's fine," Olivia answered, as she always did. "I like it."

"But you really ought to get some help," Edith insisted. "You must be there all hours…"

"Yes, but I really do enjoy it." Olivia had toyed with the idea of part-time help, but she couldn't really afford it, and what else would she do with her time?

"Still, you could get out more. Join a club in the village…" Edith looked at her hopefully. "We're always looking for bridge players on a Wednesday afternoon."

Olivia laughed and shook her head. "I'm not a patch on my mum, I'm afraid."

Yet as Edith bustled away to chat to someone else she'd seen, leaving Olivia alone, she wondered at her own reluctance to hire help. She *could* afford it if she really wanted to…and an afternoon off would surely be welcome?

She'd been living in Wychwood-on-Lea for coming on two years and she hadn't joined any village clubs or societies, hadn't made any friends besides those at Willoughby Close, and she didn't, Olivia realised with a pang, really feel as if she *belonged* in the village, outside of her shop and the people she chatted to on occasion. It was a rather depressing thought, and one that hadn't actually occurred to her before. She had friends and she was busy; it had felt like enough, until suddenly it didn't, and she didn't even know why.

"Olivia."

Simon's voice, full of warmth, had her turning, a smile blooming shyly across her face. Never mind that she still didn't know that many people in the village, here was a man she wanted to know. And judging by the happy look on Simon's face, he wanted to get to know her, as well.

"Hello—"

"I'm so glad you decided to come. Can I fetch you a drink?" He glanced at her plastic cup. "Another?"

"Oh, well, all right, then," Olivia practically stammered. She felt like a schoolgirl under Simon's warm, appreciative gaze. "You were wonderful, by the way. I love the sound of the cello."

"Thank you." He looked so pleased she couldn't keep from smiling, her heart buoyed by happiness through this little exchange. "I'll be back in a tick," he added, taking her empty cup. "Don't move."

"I won't," Olivia promised, and she didn't, smiling foolishly as Simon made his way to the drinks table and the vat of mulled wine. He'd just filled two glasses when a woman in a swing coat, her wild dark hair piled on top of her head in a messy bun, strode purposefully through the crowd and then right to Simon.

Olivia watched, her smile starting to fade, as she tapped Simon on the shoulder, and then he turned, hurriedly putting down the drinks as the woman enveloped him in a tight embrace.

It wasn't the usual side-arm hug of congratulations, but an emotional, intimate expression of affection that went on for several prolonged seconds. Olivia could see Simon's face as he wrapped his arms around the woman, his eyes closed tightly, a look of naked emotion contorting his features. Watching them, she almost felt like a voyeur from across the crowded narthex.

Finally they separated, but even then the woman gripped Simon by the shoulders, talking to him earnestly while he listened with a similar intentness, their drinks—and Olivia—forgotten. Whatever was happening between them, it was important and intense and it served as a painful and perhaps timely reminder that Olivia still didn't know him all that well, if at all.

It didn't look as if the conversation was going to finish anytime soon, and so Olivia wound her way through the crowd, grabbing her coat from an empty pew and then heading out into the cold, dark night.

The air was so sharp it nearly stole her breath, and clouds had moved over the moon, making the blackness seem almost impenetrable. The Christmas tree and fairy lights spangling the high street were all turned off, awaiting the official Turning on the Lights ceremony, and just like they'd sung in the Advent carols, the world seemed hushed and expectant, waiting...but for what?

Nothing, Olivia couldn't keep from thinking rather flatly as she walked in the dark towards home. Nothing but more of the same. And for the first time in a long while, that thought didn't fill her with optimism or happiness.

Struggling against a terrible, towering disappointment that she knew was unwarranted considering the situation, she unlocked the door to Tea on the Lea and breathed in the faint scent of cinnamon and spice from her earlier baking. It looked like the evening was shaping up to be exactly what she'd thought it would be earlier—a lot of mince pies and the company of her ornery cat. With a sigh, Olivia closed the door and locked it, and then turned towards the kitchen.

Chapter Five

TEA ON THE Lea was filled with festive smells and sights as Olivia bustled around at five o'clock on Wednesday evening, in preparation for the village's Turning on the Lights ceremony.

Mallory and Abby had offered to help, and were decked out in white T-shirts and black miniskirts, with red velvet bows in their hair as they assembled trays of various Christmas goodies—mince pies, shortbread, gingerbread, and Olivia's red velvet cupcakes decorated with holly piped in green royal icing. A huge pot of mulled wine was simmering on the stove, along with spiced apple cider for children and teetotallers. Christmas carols blasted from the speakers stuck in the corner and the shop was awash with fairy lights, holly, and red velvet ribbon. It was as Christmassy as she could make it, and with the high street filling up with families intent on seeing the switch-on, Olivia was hopeful of generating some business.

"Why didn't you do this last year?" Mallory asked as she loaded up another tray in the kitchen. Olivia had spent the last forty-eight hours elbow-deep in flour; she'd even dreamed of shortcrust pastry last night. It had been more of a nightmare, with the pastry falling apart in her hands time and time again, and she'd actually woken up in a cold sweat, relieved that it was nothing but a dream, and about pastry at that.

"I didn't think of it," she told Mallory, "and more's the pity." Last year she had been focused on Alice and Henry's wedding, and transferring the business from her mother's name to her own. She hadn't thought beyond either of those things. "Hopefully it will become a tradition now, along with the evening I'm planning next week." She'd fanned out the invitations by the front door, the red and green lettering promising plenty of Christmas treats, a quiz, and carol singing.

"It should become a tradition," Tina volunteered from her place at a table, where she was sticking cloves in several oranges to add to the spicy and festive scent of the shop. "I'm ashamed I never thought of it, for all these years."

"Mum said they've only been doing the switching-on-the-lights thing for a few years," Mallory offered. "So maybe you didn't have the opportunity."

Olivia was just glad her mum had agreed to come out for the evening. She'd resisted when Olivia had rung her on Monday, asking if she wanted to come, but then finally, after much cajoling and chivvying, she had agreed. Olivia had driven to Witney to pick her up, leaving Mallory with the awesome responsibility of taking the last batch of shortbread out on time, which she'd thankfully done.

Since she'd arrived Tina had kept busy in her corner, and Olivia had far more clove-stuck oranges than she actually needed, but at least her mum was staying busy and seemed happy. It made Olivia realise, with one of those funny little pangs, how much she *hadn't* been busy or happy in the last year and a half she'd been in the shop. How slowly but surely she'd let go of her responsibilities while Olivia had taken over, too busy really to notice how little her mum did, or how adrift she had started to seem.

"It does seem like a nice tradition," Tina said as she continued with her cloves. "Both the switching on of the lights and keeping the shop open. You've done well, Olivia. So well." She smiled wistfully, and Olivia suppressed another of those pangs.

"Thanks, Mum, but you're the one who kept this shop going for so long. It still feels much more of your place than mine." Which wasn't *entirely* true, considering how many hours Olivia spent there, but she wanted her mother to feel a part of things.

"Oh, no." Tina shook her head. "This is all yours now, Olivia."

"How is it going?" Ellie cried gaily as she came into the shop with her husband, Oliver, a bespectacled cutie who gave Olivia a charmingly bashful smile.

"Good, I think." Olivia tucked a wisp of decidedly frizzy

hair behind her ear. "We officially open our doors in..." She checked her watch. "Five minutes."

"Well, I think everything looks fab. So Christmassy. And someone said it might snow!" Someone was always saying it might snow, and occasionally it did. Olivia just smiled and then Ellie angled a little closer and dropped her voice to a rather theatrical whisper. "And what about Cupcake Man?"

Cupcake Man? Seriously? Olivia managed what she hoped was a careless shrug. "I have no idea."

"Oh." Ellie's face fell. "Hasn't he come in again?"

"Has who come in?" Mallory asked, always wanting to know the latest gossip.

Olivia busied herself with arranging a few more shortbread on an already full tray. "No one and no," she said brightly. "But hopefully the shop will be full in a few minutes!"

Thankfully Ellie took the hint and didn't press—not that there was any information for her to ferret out. Olivia hadn't seen Simon since the concert on Sunday, something she was doing her best not to find crushing. So she'd got her hopes up a little, thinking there might be a spark between them. It happened.

Clearly something was going on with the arty, elegant woman who had given him the full-on embrace at the church. They looked good together, both tall and dark and artistic-looking. She wished them well. Really.

Of course, he still could have come in and bought a cupcake each day as he'd said he would, but oh, well. The promotion seemed to be working—she'd sold all twelve on Monday and eleven on Tuesday, and most of those had been repeats of people who'd bought before and were hoping for a free cupcake at the end. Really, it was all good…or at least mostly good.

She might be disappointed that things with Simon had fizzled out before they'd even started, but so what? She still had a lot to look forward to in her life.

Olivia was spared from dwelling on it by the first rush of customers—the little shop was packed out as soon as Mallory flung open the doors, and Olivia was kept busy filling cups with mulled wine, replenishing trays, and manning the till. She'd kept the prices down to encourage custom—a pound for a cup of mulled wine and fifty pence per baked item, and she was pleased her strategy seemed to be working, as people eagerly scoffed her offerings and took the invitations from the table by the door.

She'd told herself not to keep an eye out for Simon, and yet some contrary part of her still waited—and hoped. He was, predictably, a no-show, but it helped that Ava and Jace, Alice and Henry, and Harriet and Richard all showed up, pitching in as needed, and buying plenty of pies and cakes.

"Whatever's left, I'll buy from you," Harriet promised. "I've got some of Richard's school colleagues coming over for a drinks do and I can't be bothered to bake. Besides yours are much better than anything I could manage."

"It's a deal," Olivia answered. "But I'm hoping there won't be anything left over."

A little before six o'clock everyone filed out of the shop for the lighting of the Christmas tree; Olivia had been planning on staying back but Ellie protested that she should come and close the shop for a few minutes, and then her mum insisted she'd stay.

"I can keep things going here for a little while," she said firmly. "And I don't fancy walking on those uneven cobbles in the dark. Go on, Olivia. Have some fun. I'll enjoy being in charge for a little bit."

"All right, then." Olivia untied her apron and grabbed her coat, glad to see her mother looking a bit more lively. "Thanks, Mum."

Outside people were heading in a steady stream towards the village green at the bottom of the high street. The air was full of excitement, children skipping ahead and parents laughing, everyone bundled up in bright coats and mittens, hats and scarves. The air felt crisp and cold, with a hint of the promised snow. As Olivia was pulled along with Ellie, Oliver, Abby, and Mallory, she found herself getting into the festive spirit of the thing.

She'd been so busy running around trying to make the shop look Christmassy and inviting that she hadn't actually had much time to feel Christmassy herself. Now, digging her hands deep into the pockets of her coat as she traded cheerful quips with Mallory and Abby, a happy excitement burst in her heart like a sunbeam or a snowflake. It really was the season.

On the village green everyone assembled around the massive tree; with a very small pang of uneasy guilt, Olivia noted the food stall that was doing a fairly brisk business in the same sort of fare she was offering back at the shop, with all proceeds to benefit the village cricket club. All her proceeds were going directly into her pocket. Still, her shop was halfway down the high street, a good distance from the green, and she decided there were enough pedestrians for both of them.

"Are we ready to get this party started?" someone shouted, and someone official—the head teacher of the school, Mallory said—made a big show of turning on the switch. A second later the tree lit up with an electric rainbow of colours, and the fairy lights spangling the high street lit up as well, making it look like something out of a fairy tale.

"All it needs to do is snow and everything will be perfect," Ellie said with a smile. She tilted her face to the sky, scanning for snowflakes. "It's certainly cold enough."

"Yes…" Olivia gazed around the crowded green, smiling at the sight of so many happy families, couples hand in hand…and she was happy, too. She might need a bit of forceful reminding of the fact, but it was still the truth. Her oh-so-brief fascination with Simon Blacklock had been nothing more than a blip.

And then she saw him. Her heart didn't so much as

tumble this time as freeze, suspended in her chest, as she watched him talking and laughing with someone she couldn't see. The mystery woman from Sunday in the bright, jaunty coat?

Olivia tried to look away, but somehow she couldn't. She watched as he a raked a long-fingered hand through his hair, nodding at whatever his conversational partner was saying. And then a little tousle-haired boy tackled his knees.

Olivia sucked in a hard breath as Simon reached down to unwrap the boy's arms from around his legs and then hoist him onto one hip in an easy, natural movement. The boy looked to be only four or five...and even from across the green, Olivia could see how much he looked like Simon. Dark curly hair, an impish expression, and clearly a close relationship, judging from the way the tyke was snuggling in.

Oh, she was so stupid. And yet...before that woman had accosted him in the church, it had seemed as if he was interested in her. Or had she completely misread, well, everything, and he'd just been kindly offering her a drink?

Obviously that was what had happened, because she didn't think Simon was a player, and it looked more and more like he had a family. Well. She'd already told herself it was a blip. Now she had extra, unneeded confirmation.

She was finally about to turn away when Simon glanced in her direction—and his gaze latched on to hers. For a few endless seconds Olivia felt as if the world had shrunk to this one shared look, everything around her fading out—the chatter, the lights, the tinny Christmas carols coming from the loudspeakers.

Then she forced herself to look away—and more importantly, to walk away. If she'd been feeling a bit more self-possessed, she would have gone over to Simon and said hello, let him introduce her to his family. Unfortunately, she wasn't quite there yet, and this was the best she could manage.

"Blip," she muttered under her breath. "Very, very small blip."

She walked blindly through the crowds, barely aware of where she was going, only needing some space and privacy to gather her wayward emotions together and tell them to settle down. She was halfway towards the church's covered lych gate, thankfully shrouded in shadow, when she heard someone calling her name.

"Olivia! Olivia, wait!"

Olivia turned, blinking in the gloomy darkness, to see Simon striding towards her. Her mind buzzed blankly as he came closer, stopping in front of her with a huff of breath.

"Hey." He smiled with a wryness that was both familiar and confusing. He was looking at her as he had before, as if he hadn't left her hanging on Sunday, and then not come to the shop for the last three days. But of course she was overreacting. He was a stranger. She had to keep remembering that.

"I just wanted to say…" He hesitated, looking uncertain

and a little embarrassed. "I saw you across the green and I realised what it might look like…that is, who I was with…" He trailed off and Olivia just waited, curious as to what he was trying to say and having no idea what to say herself. "The thing is," he blurted, "that little boy…he's not mine."

Okay, *that* was unexpected. Olivia tried to formulate a response but could only come up with "Right…"

"If you were wondering. And if you weren't, then I realise this conversation is exceedingly awkward and well, odd." He let out an uncertain laugh. "I just mean, you might have got the wrong end of the stick… I would understand if you had…when you saw me. And I didn't want you to think that…well, that I had a child. Or you know, other…things."

"Okay," Olivia said after a moment. She still wasn't entirely sure what he was trying to communicate, but she felt the tiniest bit hopeful that it was something good.

"I'm really explaining myself badly," Simon said with a rueful shake of his head. "All I'm trying to say is…I'm not…well, I'm single." Even in the darkness Olivia could see how much he was blushing, and now she probably was, as well. Her face was certainly starting to feel fiery, because surely there could only be one reason why he was telling her all this?

"Who were you with on Sunday?" she asked, half-wishing she hadn't mentioned Sunday, and yet still wanting to know.

"Sunday…" He frowned, and then she saw the exact

moment when he remembered what had happened, and who he was with, just as she could tell the memory pained him. It was there in the quick flinch, the shadow that flitted through his eyes. "That was Bella, my sister. After we talked, I looked around for you, but you were gone."

Olivia nodded, not wanting to explain, and not totally trusting Simon's seemingly simple explanation. His *sister*? It made sense; they had a similar look about them, and yet... Olivia had a gut instinct that it was a little more complicated than that. The exchange she'd witnessed had seemed so intense, so emotional.

She decided to take a step back, figuratively if not physically. "Well, thanks for the explanation, but I'd really better be getting back to the shop."

"Let me walk with you."

She shrugged, not wanting to argue the point, and not sure how she felt about this enigmatic man. On Sunday she'd felt, rightly or wrongly, as if she—*they*—had been on the cusp of something, and then it had all fallen flat. He'd been avoiding the shop, or so it had felt like, and yet she could hardly ask him why he hadn't bought a cupcake in the last three days. The whole thing felt a bit ridiculous.

They walked in silence up the high street; already people were trickling away from the green, heading towards home. Olivia doubted she'd get much more custom that night, and Harriet would be able to buy plenty of cakes. She couldn't keep from sighing at the thought, and Simon glanced at her.

"What's wrong?"

"Nothing, it's just been a long day." She shrugged, determined not to give in to the doldrums. "I'm ready to put my feet up and binge on a boxed set."

"Sounds like a good plan."

Had he wanted her to invite him along? Olivia had no idea what Simon wanted, what he was thinking, and suddenly she decided she was too old for these kinds of games. As they neared the shop, she stopped and turned to him.

"So, Simon, why did you want me to know you were single?"

He blinked, and then took her abrupt question in his stride. "Because I wanted to ask you out," he answered with an easy smile.

Oh. Well, then. Excitement flickered through her, and yet even so Olivia couldn't banish a stirring of unease. "You haven't been to buy a cupcake in days."

"I know." He glanced away briefly. "I meant to, but…"

She shook her head. "It's not a big deal." It really wasn't, and yet she couldn't shake the feeling that there was something Simon wasn't telling her. Something he didn't *want* to tell her. And yet she had no idea what it could be.

"Anyway," Simon said, injecting a bright note in his voice. "If you fancy a drink at The Three Pennies one night…"

Did she? Of course she did. Whatever Simon wasn't saying, and perhaps it was nothing, she still fancied a drink with him. "Yes, of course," she said. "Whenever you're free…"

"Tomorrow night?"

Excitement flickered again, stronger this time. "Yes, okay."

He smiled, and then nodded towards the shop. "Any cupcakes left?"

She nodded, smiling back. "Today was toffee apple."

She pushed open the door, blinking in the bright light of the shop as Simon followed her. Her mother had tidied up, clearing tables and tucking in chairs, but Olivia couldn't see her anywhere.

"Mum…? Are you here…?"

"Back here." Her mother sounded distressed, and with her heart leaping into her throat, Olivia hurried towards the kitchen.

"Mum…!" Her mother was slumped against the counter, cradling her arm to her chest. "What happened?"

"It was so silly of me…" Tina shook her head, tears of pain as well as shame smarting in her eyes. "I was pouring the mulled wine and I didn't see… I managed to slop it all over myself."

"Oh, Mum." Gently Olivia took hold of her mother's arm, wincing at the sight of the red, blistered burn from her wrist to her elbow. "This needs to be seen to, Mum—"

"I don't want to make a fuss—"

"It looks serious." Panic cramped her stomach as she gazed at the burn. "Let me drive you to the hospital in

Witney."

"Oh, no—"

"Please, Mum."

"Why don't I drive you?" Simon said unexpectedly. "Then you can focus on your mum, Olivia, and I can manage the driving and the parking. My car's parked just down the road."

"Oh…" Disconcerted, Olivia couldn't think how to respond. The offer was so surprising and yet also welcome. Olivia was shaken herself, and her mum needed all her attention. And, she realised, she liked the idea of having some support. "Only if you want to…" she started, trailing off uncertainly, only to have Simon give a firm nod.

"Of course I do," he said. "I'll go get my car and drive up to the front of the shop."

Chapter Six

THE WAITING ROOM of Witney Hospital's A&E was crowded with a variety of illnesses and injuries, and despite Olivia insisting on the severity of her mother's burn—not to mention her age—the nurse didn't give them any preferential treatment. Not that Olivia would have wanted it, precisely, but she still felt anxious, perhaps more anxious than the situation warranted.

Her mother had always been her bedrock, she reflected as the three of them sat in hard plastic seats in the waiting room. For her whole life, her mother had solidly *been* there, utterly dependable, always warm and welcoming. And yet now, with the painful benefit of hindsight, Olivia could see that her mum had started...*fading* a little in the last two years, since she'd moved back home.

It had happened in such small increments that she hadn't really noticed; she'd been busy with the shop, and she'd seen what she'd wanted to see. But now she felt as if a dark mist was creeping over the landscape of her life and she didn't even understand it, or why she was so worried. It was just a burn…wasn't it? It had to be.

The touch of Simon's hand on her own startled her out of her worried reverie. "Try not to worry," he said, his voice gentle. "I'm sure she'll be seen soon."

"Thank you," Olivia murmured. She was grateful for Simon driving them to Witney; her mum had been agitated and Olivia had concentrated on trying to comfort her. She'd felt too dazed to drive, and yet now that they were here and she was starting to feel a little bit more like herself, she realised it was undeniably awkward to have Simon Blacklock here, kindly and well meaning—as well as a potential date— but still a stranger. And who even knew how long they'd be waiting? A crowded A&E in the pre-Christmas flu season? It could be hours, maybe even all night.

"If you want to go back," Olivia offered in a low voice, "please feel free. I don't know how long we'll be, and I can always call a cab."

"I'm not bothered," Simon replied. "I don't have any-where better to be."

"Don't you?" She was curious, and it felt like a much-needed distraction to wonder about someone other than her mum. "Why not?"

Simon shrugged. "I've only been in Wychwood for a few months. I don't know many people, haven't got much going on." He sounded a bit like her, give or take another year or two. He smiled at her, his eyes crinkling at the corners. "I'm happy to be here, Olivia."

Olivia nodded, believing him, yet it still felt like a big ask, and it put their relationship, or lack of it, on a whole other, awkward footing. She turned to her mum, who was cradling her arm, her gaze unfocused.

"How are you holding up, Mum? Can I get you anything?"

"I just want to go home," Tina said, looking as if she were fighting tears. "I don't need all this bother."

"I know it's difficult," Olivia said as gently as she could, "but it's a bad burn and it needs proper looking at, Mum. We'll be seen soon, I'm sure." Tina just shook her head, and Olivia bit her lip.

Her mother's behaviour seemed so out of character—and yet it had been *in* character for the last few months. Olivia just hadn't wanted to see it, had always brushed aside the faint unease she'd felt when visiting her mother in Witney. And she still wanted to brush it aside, insist that once her mother's arm was bandaged, everything would be okay, because any alternative was too difficult to consider.

"Tina James?" a nurse called, and Olivia rose with relief.

"That's us, Mum." She helped Tina up, taking her good arm, and they walked towards the doors that led to the A&E ward while Simon stayed in the waiting room.

A few seconds later they were settled in a small, curtained cubicle with a brisk-seeming nurse sitting across from Tina.

"You burned yourself, did you? How did it happen?"

"Oh, it was nothing, it's so silly," Tina said, trying her

best to sound dismissive. "I was ironing and I touched the hot plate…"

Shock jolted through Olivia at this admission. "Mum," she said as gently as she could, trying to keep the alarm from her voice, "you burned it on the mulled wine—didn't you?" She exchanged a questioning glance with the nurse and gave a little shake of her head. What was going on?

"Oh yes…" Tina bit her lip and then nodded. "Yes, that's what I meant."

"Let me take a look at it, then." Tina held out her arm and the nurse examined the angry red burn that had already blistered. "This does look painful," she murmured with a sympathetic smile for Tina. "I just need to clean the affected area and then we'll put a sterile dressing on it, all right?"

"I don't want to cause any trouble…" Tina began and the nurse's smile deepened.

"You aren't, love, promise. That's what we're here for." She turned Tina's arm over and then paused. Olivia craned her head to see what she was looking at. "It looks like you've burned yourself before," she remarked casually. "On your wrist?"

"Oh, that, yes. That was the iron."

Olivia looked at the still-red mark, her stomach and mind both churning. When had her mother burned herself? And why hadn't she told Olivia? Of course, her mum didn't mention every little thing that happened, but the burn still looked painful and two burns in the course of a few days…

"Right, well, let's get you cleaned up," the nurse said briskly. Olivia watched, her mind still spinning, as the nurse cleaned and bandaged the burn. "Best if you see your GP in twenty-four hours to have it looked at and the dressing changed, all right, love?" She paused, her gaze moving to Olivia. "I'll just have the consultant come in for a moment so you can have a chat."

"We don't need to chat," Tina began in protest, but the nurse had already left the cubicle with a rattle of the curtain rings.

"It's fine, Mum," Olivia said, trying to sound upbeat. "The doctor most likely just wants to check you're all right."

"I know I'm all right," Tina said irritably. "Honestly, such a fuss." She half-rose from her chair. "Let's just go home, Olivia. I really want to go home."

"Mum." As gently as she could, Olivia put her hand on her mother's shoulder and steered her back into the chair. "Let's just wait and see what he says, okay? You want the best care."

Tina continued to fret, and Olivia's own agitation grew as they waited another twenty minutes for the consultant on call to come in. Finally he did, looking far too young and cheerful.

"Hello, there." He scanned Tina's notes quickly before sitting in front of her with a kindly smile. "The nurse has suggested you be referred to your GP for a few tests."

"Tests? I've burned myself," Tina retorted, sounding far

bolshier than Olivia had ever heard her sound before. "What kind of tests do I need?"

The doctor's eyes were kind as he answered steadily, "The nurse suggested it might be advisable that you have a cognitive test. It's a simple one, done at the GP's, and it only takes five minutes." He glanced at Olivia. "If you ring tomorrow, you might get an early appointment or a cancellation."

"Tomorrow…" Olivia's mind spun and spun. A cognitive test? What was the doctor *saying*? She glanced at her mother, whose irritation had vanished; she now seemed to be sinking into herself, her head and gaze both lowered.

"All right, then," she said quietly, and panic seized Olivia, a visceral clawing of her insides. Her mother looked almost as if she'd given up, and Olivia wasn't even sure what was going on.

She wanted to ask the doctor about the cognitive test and what it meant, but she was also afraid to. Finally she found the words. "What is this cognitive test?" she asked shakily. "What would it be testing for?"

"It's an early assessment to check for memory loss and signs of dementia," he answered and Olivia nearly staggered. *Dementia…?*

"But my mother burned herself, she didn't…" She trailed off, remembering how Tina had mistaken the cause of the burn, and a dozen other details besides. How fretful she'd seemed. How she didn't want to go out. How she'd lost interest in so many things she'd once loved—the shop, baking, bridge, even Christmas.

The doctor must have seen the dawning terror in her eyes for he said gently, "It's just a test. A check. Your GP can take it from there and who knows, it may be nothing. But it's important to rule things out."

Or rule things *in*? Olivia murmured something in agreement, and then she was helping her mum into her coat and they were walking into the brightly lit waiting room, Simon rising expectantly as they approached him, but Olivia felt too dazed to say anything.

"Everything all right?" he asked brightly and it took her a few seconds to respond.

"Yes…the burn is bandaged. We need to go to the GP tomorrow to have the dressing checked."

"I don't—" Tina began, but Olivia shook her head firmly.

"No, Mum. You do."

Simon was kind enough to drop Tina off at her flat, and then wait while Olivia saw her inside, making her a cup of tea and then settling her in bed before she left.

"I don't want you to worry, Olivia," Tina said just as she was about to bid her good night. Olivia paused, one hand on the bedroom door.

"Of course I'll worry, Mum," she said. "I love you. I want you to be well."

Tina shook her head. "It would be different if you were

married and had your own family," she said, making Olivia flinch a little. "But you're all alone. It's not right for you to have to bear the burden of—of taking care of me."

"You did the same for me," Olivia reminded her rather fiercely. "For all my life. And it hasn't come to that yet, Mum. It's just a test."

Tina smiled sadly and Olivia was jolted to her core. The look in her mum's eyes said as plainly as could be that she knew what the result of the test was going to be.

Back in the car Olivia slid into the passenger seat, her body and heart both aching. It was nearly ten o'clock, and Simon had been waiting in the car for almost an hour.

"I'm sorry about that," she said dully. "I didn't realise how long I was taking."

"It's no problem." He started the car and then pulled out into the dark, empty street. Olivia leaned her head against the seat and closed her eyes, fighting a fear and grief that felt as if it could overwhelm her. "Do you want to talk about it?" Simon asked quietly, making her jerk a little bit.

"Talk about it? Do you know…?"

"I don't know anything, only that something seems to be going on that's more than an accident at the stove." He paused. "But you don't have to tell me if you don't want to. I really don't mean to pry."

"I know. Thanks." She took a shuddering breath, wanting someone to confide in, but unsure whether it should be Simon. *I barely know him* seemed to be her constant refrain, and yet he was the one who had been there when her mum had had her accident, and he'd been the one to drive them to the hospital and wait while she was seen.

"The doctor referred her to the GP for a cognitive test," she blurted. It almost felt like a relief to say it somehow, to share it. "I have to ring tomorrow."

"A cognitive test." Simon repeated the words neutrally.

"Yes." While her mum had been in the loo Olivia had searched on her phone and scrolled through the ten warning signs of dementia, her heart plummeting with each one. *Difficulty completing normal tasks...confusion...apathy...changes in mood...difficulty with spatial orientation, which can result in seeming clumsiness...* and accidents. Burns. Olivia swallowed hard. "It's a test for dementia," she clarified, and Simon nodded.

"Yes."

"I think I was afraid of something like this ever since she burned herself," Olivia admitted. "All evening, while we were waiting, I felt this panic that didn't make sense if it really was just a burn. But of course it isn't."

"You don't know that..."

"No, but I think she does. The look on her face..." Olivia shook her head, her throat closing up. She didn't want to lose it in front of Simon. They hadn't even gone on their date yet.

"I'm sorry, Olivia," he said, his voice so heartfelt it made her eyes sting. "I really am sorry."

"Thank you."

They didn't talk for the rest of the journey back to Wychwood-on-Lea, which was a relief. Simon parked in front of Tea on the Lea, and when Olivia turned to bid him farewell, as well as a huge thank you, he gave her a lopsided smile.

"I'll see you to the door."

She fumbled with the key, feeling both awkward in Simon's presence and yet desperately not wanting to be alone. As she stepped into the shop Dr Jekyll let out a yowl and jumped into her arms, making Olivia let out a screech of surprise even as she instinctively clasped him to her chest. She stumbled back into Simon, who steadied her, his hands warm and solid on her shoulders. Her back collided with his chest.

"Sorry..." she mumbled, embarrassed and off balance, her arms full of aggrieved feline. "He hasn't been fed, poor cat." Dr Jekyll deigned to show his displeasure by digging his claws deep into Olivia's arms and she let out a little yelp.

"Sorry," she said again as she stepped away from Simon. "He's a bit of a crazy cat." Which was an understatement. "He's called Dr Jekyll."

"Ah. The name says it all, really."

"Yes. I'd better get him some food." She moved towards the stairs in the back of the shop that led up to her flat, realising belatedly that Simon hadn't actually left. She turned around and he gave her an awkward smile.

"Sorry, I'll go. I just wanted to make sure you were okay on your own."

"Ye-es…" Olivia began, but to her mortification, her voice wobbled all over the place and ended on something that sounded alarmingly close to a sob.

"Oh, Olivia." With his face full of sympathy, Simon walked towards her and then put his arms around her, cat and all. Dr Jekyll let out an indignant yowl and jumped out of her arms, leaving Olivia free to put her arms around Simon, which she realised she very much wanted to do.

There was nothing romantic about their hug; it was a gesture solely of comfort and compassion, understanding and sympathy, and Olivia needed it very, very much.

She breathed in the scent of Simon—frosty air and wool scarf, a hint of lemony aftershave. She closed her eyes, savouring the feel of his arms around her, his body next to hers. When had she last been hugged properly, not just a quick side-arm or excited squeeze by one of her friends? She couldn't even remember, but she knew now that she'd missed it. A lot.

Eventually, though, she knew she had to break the hug; Dr Jekyll made that obvious when he wound his way between their legs, yowling plaintively.

"Sorry," she mumbled, stepping back from Simon's embrace. She wasn't quite sure what she was saying sorry for. The cat? The hug? The whole evening? Or just the fact that she was clearly on the verge of losing it completely?

"It's okay, Olivia." Simon's voice was gentle. "It's fine."

She drew in a shuddery breath. "It's just...it's always been my mum and me," she said, trying to explain why this was affecting her so deeply. "We've been a team since...well, since forever." Another shuddery breath; saying even this much was harder than she'd thought. "I can't imagine it any way else." And yet she knew in her heart, in her very bones, that it had already changed without her realising it. Already her mum wasn't the same. *They* weren't the same. "That's why it's so hard," she finished. "But thank you for taking us to the hospital, and waiting while I settled my mum. I really appreciate it."

"You don't have to keep thanking me." Simon smiled wryly, a touch of sadness lingering in his eyes. "You're sure you're okay?"

No, she wasn't okay, but she couldn't ask any more of Simon now. "I'll be okay," she said. "I'll ring the doctor tomorrow."

He hesitated, looking uncertain. "Of course, you don't have to come out for a drink tomorrow night, considering..."

She'd completely forgotten about their would-be date. She felt as if they were in a whole other place now after this evening. "No, I'd like to go. It will be nice to do something different." She tried to smile. "If you're still up for it, that is."

"I am."

"Okay, then. The Three Pennies at seven?"

"Sounds like a plan."

They gazed at each other for a moment, the silence that stretched between them feeling both comfortable and strange, as if they were communicating something without words.

"I'd better head off, then," Simon said, and turned towards the door. "See you tomorrow, Olivia."

"Yes, see you tomorrow." She waited until he'd disappeared down the street, into the darkness, before she locked the door and turned off the lights, heading upstairs to her flat with Dr Jekyll hard on her heels, eager for his dinner.

Chapter Seven

THE NEXT MORNING Olivia rang the local GP, muttering a prayer of thanks under her breath when a last-minute cancellation meant her mother could be seen later that morning. She rang Harriet next, asking her to cover the shop for an hour or two, something she'd done on occasion in the past, when it couldn't be avoided.

Olivia had never liked asking favours from people; perhaps it stemmed from her childhood, when she and her mum had been their own secure, and somewhat isolated, unit. Mum had always been proud not to need anyone else, even though she'd loved providing baking and a listening ear to whoever came her way. It was a one-sided offer, to be the listener and sympathiser rather than the listened to, the one who needed a bit of compassion, and Olivia had inherited that tendency, the drive for self-sufficiency and security. Better to be needed than to need.

Thankfully Harriet had been quick to agree, and she strolled into the shop at quarter to eleven, looking worried.

"Is everything okay, Olivia? What's up with your mum?"

"Just a burn that needs checking." Olivia didn't want to go into the cognitive testing bit just yet; it felt like a betrayal of her mother, and it wasn't really her news to share. "Thanks for helping out."

"Of course, I'm delighted to. I would more often if you wanted me to."

"I know." Olivia gave her a rather guilty smile, knowing it was her emotional issue that kept her from leaning on her friends more. Harriet glanced around the shop.

"This place really does look fab, so Christmassy. I love the mistletoe." She glanced at the cake stand in the front window. "What's the cupcake for today, then?"

"Raspberry cheesecake." Which might have been a bit more miss than hit, but Olivia was trying for a wide variety of flavours.

"It looks delicious. Are those crystallised raspberries on top?"

"Yes, and a bit of red glitter to make it that much more festive."

"You do such an amazing job." Harriet looked at her seriously. "You deserve massive success, Olivia."

"Thanks." Whether she would get it or not was another matter, but for once Olivia didn't have financial worries in the back of her mind. The cupcakes had been picking up, and staying open for the tree-lighting ceremony had been a definite plus. She'd had more inquiries about the evening do she was planning next week, as well. In any case, it was her mother she was worried about today.

"And what about Cupcake Man?" Harriet asked. "Has he come in again?"

Olivia rolled her eyes, simply because the question was so lovably predictable. Ellie had texted her about "Cupcake Man" that morning, and Ava had asked her about him when she'd picked up a coffee and muffin before jetting off to work. Olivia hadn't told either of them about her drink with Simon, mainly because she didn't want to make it into a bigger deal than it actually was. Now, under Harriet's beady eye, she found she couldn't quite dissemble.

"Actually, he has a name, and we're going out for a drink tonight."

"Oh, wow!" Harriet clapped her hands, genuinely delighted. "So what is his name, out of interest?"

Olivia hesitated for a second, uncertain whether to unleash her friends' inquisitiveness on her fledgling love life. "Simon Blacklock."

"Simon…" A funny look came over Harriet's face, making Olivia's fragile hopes start to waver.

"Why are you looking like that?"

"Like what?" Harriet blustered, and Olivia pursed her lips.

"Like you've just tasted something sour. What is it? Do you know him?"

"I don't know him exactly…" Harriet began, and Olivia's stomach roiled unpleasantly. This was sounding worse and worse.

"So what do you know?"

"It's just hearsay and rumours, really," Harriet said hurriedly, which only made Olivia feel even more worried. She'd *known* there had been something Simon had been holding back. Of course it was all too good to be true.

"Rumours," she repeated flatly. "From where?"

"School. He's the peripatetic music teacher for the primary school, as well as a couple of others in the area. Didn't you know that?"

"No, we hadn't got that far. I know he plays the cello," Olivia answered a bit defensively, because Harriet had sort of made it sound as if she should have known. As if she shouldn't go out with a man for a drink without knowing his occupation.

"He only started in September. He's living with his sister, who has kids at the school. A boy in year two, I think, and another in nursery."

"Yes, I know that." Sort of. She knew he had a sister and a nephew. "That hardly seems objectionable, though."

"Nooo…" Harriet sounded so uncharacteristically hesitant that Olivia felt a sudden, very real clutch of fear.

"Don't tell me," she said quickly. "I don't want to know. Not like this. It's not fair to Simon. He's not a serial killer or something, is he?"

"Not a serial killer," Harriet allowed, in a tone that suggested he was somewhere a little bit beneath that. *Good grief.*

Olivia turned away, not trusting the expression on her face, and busied herself with wiping the counter of crumbs that had scattered there after she'd cut into the Victoria sponge cake.

"Sorry, I don't mean to pour cold water all over your excitement."

Except, of course, she already had. "It's fine," Olivia said, even though it wasn't. It probably wasn't reasonable, but she felt a little miffed with Harriet for reacting the way she had, even as she battled a deepening unease over whatever it was Harriet—and Simon—weren't saying.

Harriet bit her lip, looking both guilty and miserable. "I shouldn't have said anything…"

No, she really shouldn't have. "It's fine," Olivia said firmly. "Now let me show you how the cupcake promotion works."

Ten minutes later Olivia was driving towards Witney, the rolling fields on either side of the road sparkling with frost on a crisp and sunny winter's morning, the Lea River glittering alongside. The sight of the Cotswolds in all of their natural glory made Olivia's spirits lift a little, even as she dreaded what lay ahead.

Last night, after Simon had left, she'd done an Internet search on these types of tests and cringed inwardly at how patronising they seemed, even though she knew they weren't intended to be. But drawing a clock? Recalling the date, or an address you'd be told moments before? Of course her mother could do those things, and it was an insult to her to think otherwise.

And yet…why did Olivia feel dread rather than relief? What was she so afraid of?

Her mother was waiting outside the building as Olivia pulled up. She sat on a stone bench, her gloved hands folded in her lap, her coat zipped up to her chin. She looked remarkably composed, more so than Olivia had seen her in a while, and she felt a flicker of hope, even though she couldn't articulate what it was exactly that she was hoping for.

"Hey, Mum." She jumped out of the car and hurried around to open the passenger side.

"Thank you, darling, but I'm not an invalid. Not yet." Her mother's voice was tart but she was smiling.

"Sorry, just trying to help."

"I know." As Olivia climbed back into the driver's side her mother reached over and patted her hand. "I fear, Olivia, that this is going to be much harder for you than it is for me."

Her stomach plunged unpleasantly at that quietly stated remark. "What do you mean, Mum?"

"I knew this was coming. I tried to pretend it wasn't, but I knew all the same." Tina gave her a sidelong glance. "I'm afraid that you didn't."

Olivia swallowed hard, keeping her gaze straight ahead as she navigated the narrow road out of Witney. "Do you mean you knew you were having trouble with your memory?"

"Yes, among other things."

Pain lanced through her, along with fear. "Why didn't you tell me?"

"I didn't want to worry you, and I didn't want to acknowledge it out loud, or even to myself. We can all be quite good at self-deception when we choose to."

"Oh, Mum."

"It's all right." Tina squared her shoulders. "I've lived a good life. I've followed my dreams—in having you, in opening Tea on the Lea. I don't regret anything."

A lump was forming in Olivia's throat with every word her mother spoke. "Don't make it sound as if—as if you're *dying*, Mum."

"I know I'm not dying," Tina said briskly. "Yet, anyway."

"Mum—"

"But things are going to change," her mother cut across her, her voice gentle but firm. "They already have, even if we've both closed our eyes to it."

Olivia struggled to know how to respond. Yes, they'd changed, but how could her mother be having such a calm and knowledgeable conversation about the decline of her own mind? It didn't make sense.

"Let's see what the doctor says," she said finally, and her mother just smiled.

Olivia hadn't been to the GP very often since moving to

Wychwood—a chest cold once and her tri-annual cervical smear—but now as she sat on one of the vinyl-padded chairs she took in the noticeboard full of messages for memory clinics and dementia support groups, often accompanied by photos of cheerful-looking seniors and chirpy slogans such as "I Live One Day at a Time" and "Memories are Worth Fighting For." They made her want to cry. She so wasn't ready for this.

"Tina James?" The nurse at the door to the examination rooms was smiling and friendly as both Olivia and her mother rose and followed her down the hall.

"So you've been referred for a cognitive test," the GP, one Olivia hadn't met before, asked as he scanned her mother's notes on his computer. "After receiving a burn on your forearm?"

"Yes." Tina sat in the chair next to his desk, her coat and bag on her lap. Olivia sat in the plastic chair opposite, everything inside her wound far too tightly.

"And do you feel you've been having problems with your memory?" The doctor gave her mother a kind but direct look.

"I think I may have been. Of course, it's difficult to say. It's so easy to excuse little lapses, blame it on age."

"And how old are you?"

"Seventy-three." Her mother's chin tilted upwards a notch. "Seventy-four in March."

"Memory loss or confusion is not actually a normal part

of ageing," the doctor said kindly. "So if you are experiencing those symptoms, it is important to get tested."

"Which is why we're here." A steely note entered Tina's voice. "To determine if I am in fact, losing my mind."

The doctor looked as if he wanted to argue with her choice of phrasing, but then he smiled and inclined his head. "Part of the testing process is to rule out other options. Why don't we go through your health history?"

Olivia tried to relax as he took Tina through her medical history, and then finally turned away from his computer. "Shall we get started, then?"

Tina gave a rather regal nod, and Olivia had to keep from clenching her fists and gritting her teeth as the doctor went through a test similar to the one she'd found online, asking her mum to recall today's date, which she could, and then draw a clock face on the pad of paper he pushed towards her.

Olivia watched, holding her breath, as her mother carefully drew a wavering circle, and then hesitated before filling in the numbers.

"Sorry, sorry," she muttered as she scratched out the nine, which had been in the place of the six, and put it where it belonged. The doctor watched impassively and Olivia had to bite her lips to keep from saying something pointless and unhelpful.

Anyone could mix up a six and a nine. It was *normal*. She'd done it on occasion. Then the doctor asked Tina to recall the address he'd told her at the beginning of the test, and Olivia watched with a sinking heart as her mother's brow crinkled.

"Yes, of course I remember that…it was…let me see, it was…" She paused, pursing her lips, her eyes scrunched up with the effort.

It was fifty-one Woodford Close, Mum, Olivia wanted to shout. *You said it after him, twice! Come on!*

"Something to do with…" Her mother trailed off and then shook her head, her expression turning resolute and rather stony. "I'm sorry. I can't remember."

"That's all right." The doctor spoke easily, as if this wasn't a big deal, but Olivia knew it was. It had to be. "It was fifty-one Woodford Close. Does that ring a bell?"

"Oh, yes, of course." Tina nodded. "Fifty-one Woodford Close. Now I remember." Except Olivia didn't think she did.

"Well." The doctor sat back, his hands folded. "As you probably realise, you had a few issues with some parts of the test."

"Yes." Tina pressed her lips together.

"I think the best thing to do is leave it for a few weeks, and then take you through another test, perhaps after Christmas, to see how you're getting on. In the meantime I'll schedule you for a blood test so we can rule out any other options." He gestured to her arm. "The nurse will change the dressing on your arm before you go."

They'd had their ten minutes of time, and they were now

kindly but firmly ushered out of the GP's office. Olivia felt strangely numb, and Tina looked composed.

"That wasn't as terrible as I thought," she said as they waited to see the nurse. "Although I can't believe I forgot how to draw a clock."

"Anyone can get sixes and nines confused, Mum—"

Tina gave her a sharp look. "Don't make excuses for me, Olivia. We're past that now, I think."

"Still, he wants to do more tests…" Olivia faltered at her mother's steely look, then rallied again. "I just don't want to throw in the towel at the first opportunity, Mum. Let's wait and see how the next few tests go."

Tina nodded in seeming agreement, but Olivia felt as if her mother was just humouring her. She'd already made up her mind about what was going on.

An hour later, having dropped her mother off back at home, Olivia returned to Tea on the Lea feeling mixed-up inside, a tangle of hope and fear. Harriet looked up from the till as she came in.

"We've had a run on cupcakes! Apparently word is getting around."

"Have you?" Olivia was pleasantly surprised. It was only one o'clock in the afternoon; the cupcakes usually sold later in the day.

"Yes, a mum came in to buy six for a dinner party she's having tonight. And someone else bought two…"

"Are there any left?" Olivia couldn't keep a note of anxiety from her voice, and of course Harriet picked up on it.

"Oh, yes. There's still two left. I wouldn't have sold the last one, don't you worry. I know you need to save one for your cupcake man."

Olivia didn't want to get talking about that again. "He has a name, remember."

"Yes, I remember. About that, Olivia…"

She held up a hand to forestall any of Harriet's bumbled apologies or worse, warnings. "Let's not talk about it, Harriet—"

"No, I don't want to. I just want to tell you to ignore me. I shouldn't have said anything, and I don't know anything, not really—"

Despite her obviously good intentions, Harriet was still making it worse. "I know," Olivia cut her off, hoping she would finally drop it. "It's fine. I'm just going to let Simon speak for himself."

Harriet's eyes rounded. "So you're going to ask him?"

Ask him *what*? "No, I'm going to let the conversation unfold naturally," Olivia said, holding on to her patience with effort. "And act like we never had this conversation."

Harriet finally looked as if she were getting the message and she nodded, abashed. "Right. Sorry. How's your mum, anyway? Is the burn healing all right?"

The burn was just about the least of Olivia's worries, but she still didn't feel like sharing what was going on with Harriet, even though she'd already told some of it to Simon last night. "Yes, it's healing nicely," she answered. "Thanks for minding the shop."

Harriet left a few minutes later, and Olivia bustled around, tidying up, rearranging the cakes, and generally trying to keep busy. She turned on some Christmas carols to lift her mood, wanting to get back into the holiday spirit, but after a little the cheerful noise just grated on her and she turned it off.

Two elderly ladies came in for afternoon tea, and Olivia served them, watching them surreptitiously. They looked older than her mum, and *they* didn't have dementia. They were both sharp as tacks, exchanging pointed comments about the village's flower guild.

Why her mum? Why *her*? And what was going to happen now? What was the future going to look like for both of them?

Back in the kitchen, tidying up at the end of the day, Olivia told herself to get a grip. She was nearly forty years old. She ran her own business, lived her own life. This wasn't the end of her world. *But was it the end of her mother's?*

And, she realised as she flipped the sign to closed, Simon hadn't even come in for his cupcake.

Upstairs Dr Jekyll was thankfully feeling friendly, and Olivia ate her mug of noodles for dinner with the fluffy cat nestled in her lap, trying to suppress the stab of loneliness that kept attacking her unawares.

She wasn't used to it; she'd always liked her own company. But now, with her mother's diagnosis in the offing, Olivia couldn't keep from being painfully aware of her single state. At least she had drinks with Simon to look forward to, and whatever the rest of the evening would bring.

Chapter Eight

THE THREE PENNIES had its usual clusters of well-heeled villagers scattered around the low-ceilinged room as Olivia stepped across the threshold, ducking her head under the ancient oak beam. Bing Crosby was on low volume, his melodious voice caressing the syllables of "White Christmas," heard over the murmured conversations and few bursts of laughter.

Olivia scanned the crowd for Simon, trying not to feel self-conscious or look nervous. She'd spent over an hour trying to pitch her look between made an effort and trying too hard. Wearing a crimson jumper, skinny jeans, and knee-high leather boots, her hair ·tamed into natural-looking waves—well, ish—she hoped she'd succeeded.

"Olivia." Simon rose from a cosy table in the back of the room and Olivia smiled and started forward, her heart feeling as if it were bumping against her ribs. Simon was in his usual charmingly semi-dishevelled state—hair a bit too long, corduroy blazer decidedly battered, with a button-down shirt and faded jeans. He looked scrumptious.

She came to a stop in front of him, unsure of the protocol. She'd never been one for air kissing, despite her years in London where mwah-mwah was the usual greeting, and anything more than that felt like too much, anything less— like a handshake—too formal. In the end, they simply smiled and stared at each other before Simon gestured towards the bar.

"What may I get you to drink?"

"Um…a glass of white wine, please."

"Be back in a mo." Olivia settled herself in her seat as Simon went to the bar. She glanced around the pub but thankfully didn't see anyone she knew, which was always a danger in Wychwood-on-Lea. She didn't fancy someone coming in to the shop tomorrow with a beady eye and a knowing look, wanting the low-down on her one date night since she'd moved to the village.

"Here we are." Simon reappeared with a glass of white for her and a pint of bitter for himself. He put the drinks on the table and then sat opposite her, smiling wryly. "So. We made it."

"Cheers." They clinked glasses and Olivia took a sip. "Funnily enough," she said once she'd put her glass down, "I don't actually know that much about you."

Was she imagining the guarded look on Simon's face? She must be. "I suppose you don't." Which wasn't exactly an invitation to learn more.

"You're a music teacher?" she asked, before she realised

she wouldn't have known that if Harriet hadn't said anything. Now she knew she wasn't imagining that guarded look.

"Yes…"

"My friend has kids at the local school," Olivia explained, half in apology for no doubt seeming stalkerish. "When I mentioned your name, she said she knew you."

"Ah." Simon's expression relaxed a bit, but he still looked watchful. "Do her children take music lessons?"

"Umm…I think her ten-year-old Will takes piano. What do you teach?"

"Cello and violin." He smiled ruefully.

"Right." She took another sip of wine; why did Harriet's bombshell, or lack of it, this morning now feel like a hurdle she had to leap over, a mountain she had to overcome? She'd been looking forward to this evening, but in some ways it already felt, if not ruined, then at least hampered.

"What about you?" Simon asked. "What did you do before you moved to this lovely village?"

"I lived in London, working in marketing and development for a small not-for-profit."

"What kind of not-for-profit?"

Now Olivia was the one smiling self-consciously. "An organisation that provides undergarments and sanitary products for girls and women in developing countries who have difficulty gaining access to them. I know, I know, it's a bit of a conversation stopper."

"Not at all," Simon said, rallying after a second of looking a bit nonplussed. "That sounds like a very worthy cause."

"It is," Olivia agreed, "but people don't really like talking about it all that much. Anyway." She let out a breath. "After nearly fifteen years in the same sector, I was ready for a change. Is that why you moved here from London? For a change?"

"Yes, in a way. I needed one, at least."

Needed one? Olivia knew she needed to stop thinking everything Simon said was suspect. *Why* had Harriet said anything? And yet even before she had, Olivia had wondered. It felt like there was *something* Simon wasn't saying, but she could hardly ask him what it was.

"Anyway." He smiled in his wry, charming way, his grey-green eyes lighting up. "Enough about that. Tell me something about you that doesn't involve cupcakes or sanitary products."

Olivia nearly spat out her wine. "Now that's one I haven't heard before."

"I only meant, not about work," Simon said with a rakish grin. "I want to know about you. Where did you grow up?"

"Middlesbrough. Not exactly the garden of England."

"Respectable enough. Happy families?"

"Yes, if not the usual one. My dad scarpered when I was two." She spoke matter-of-factly, slightly offhand, as she always did when people asked about her father.

Simon grimaced, a look of sympathy in his eyes. "I'm sorry."

"It's fine. My mum did the job for both of them."

"Which makes what's happening now all the harder."

"Well, yes." She'd told him something of that before, and of course he'd remembered. "I suppose it would feel a bit different if I were married," she said, and then realised how that sounded. "I mean…that's what Mum said. She doesn't want to burden me when I'm on my own, the only one to cope with what's happening."

"That's understandable." Thankfully Simon didn't seem fazed by her marriage comment. Hopefully he hadn't thought the subtext was she needed to snag a man so she could deal with her ailing mother. What a way to kill a first date. "Have you ever come close?" he asked lightly.

"To what?"

"Marriage. Kids. All that."

"No, not really." She hesitated, wondering how far she wanted to delve into her decidedly uninteresting romantic history, and then decided why not? At her age she should put all her cards on the table, and really, there weren't that many. "I had a serious boyfriend for a few years about ten years ago. We talked about it, but it never felt right. And after that everything was pretty casual." Which made her sound as if she hooked up all the time, which was so far from the truth it was ludicrous. "I mean, a couple of dates here and there. Mainly there."

Simon gave a rueful laugh. "I suppose I'm the same."

"No one serious?"

"Similar to you. I was engaged about fifteen years ago, in my twenties, to another musician. We met in uni and then she got a gig travelling the world with an orchestra. It was for eighteen months, and I thought we'd survive it, but then I got a 'Dear John' email from Singapore. It wasn't meant to be."

"No, that's how I've always thought. If I'd really want to get married, I would have done. I wouldn't have been so picky."

"And now?" Simon asked, his gaze serious enough to make her squirm a little. "How do you feel about all that now?"

Gulp. Was this really the kind of question to ask on a first date? But of course it was; neither of them were getting any younger. No point in wasting time if they wanted different things in life.

"Honestly?" Olivia rotated her wineglass by its stem as she considered his question—and her answer. "I don't know. In London I was always happy enough, being the honorary auntie, the godmother, the best friend."

"All supporting roles."

She was gratified he got it so quickly. "Exactly. And that really suited me fine. I liked having my freedom—my own place, Saturdays to do with as I chose, always able to decide what I want to eat or watch on telly."

"There are definitely some perks to the single life."

"Yes." She took a deep breath. "But I'm turning forty in a few months and things are starting to feel different, I suppose—with my mum and also my friends all having kids and busy lives. Living in Wychwood isn't actually a swinging singles paradise, not that I'd want that scene."

"True. So what do you want out of life now?"

"Wow, deep question."

"No point pussyfooting around, is there? We don't spend enough time pondering the deep questions, in my opinion."

"No, I don't suppose we do." Olivia took a sip of wine, considering. "I suppose I'm a little scared," she admitted, surprised at how vulnerable she was being—and yet Simon had already seen her vulnerable, back in the hospital and afterwards.

"Scared of what?"

"The future. Living the rest of it alone. I've got Dr Jekyll of course, but as you know he's a changeable creature."

"There's still time, though, isn't there?" He smiled wryly. "I'm forty-one in April and I'm still hoping there is."

"Time for what, exactly?" Olivia decided to be direct. "Because in terms of the whole bumps-and-babies thing, there probably isn't, for me." Which perhaps was too much information, but she knew some men set a lot of store by these things. Back in London, she'd seen far too many men her own age preferring a younger, more fertile model.

"I suppose it depends. I can't say I'm an expert, but in

any case I wasn't speaking so much of kids as life partner. Love, marriage, that sort of thing."

"Ah. Well, here's hoping."

"Yes." His voice dropped a notch, taking on a not-so-subtle meaning that made Olivia's insides fizz. "Here's hoping."

Thankfully then they kept the conversation lighter, talking about village life and art and music, and then Simon fetched a pair of menus in case they wanted any food.

Olivia realised she was enjoying herself; she'd let go of her nerves and worries and was simply revelling in being with someone who was witty and interesting and attractive, and more importantly, interested in her. She loved how Simon gave her his full attention, his gaze both warm and alert, so clearly listening to everything she said. It was a rare gift in any person, to be so fully present and involved.

They ordered a couple of starters and shared them; Olivia didn't even mind gnawing at a buffalo wing in front of him, getting sauce on her chin in the process, and no doubt shreds of meat between her teeth.

"So, do you think you'll stay in Wychwood long-term?" she asked after they'd polished off a plate of wings as well as another of nachos.

"I think for the time being, yes. It's good to be close to my sister, and I was getting priced out of London anyway."

"You live with your sister?" Olivia asked, and that surprised, slightly guarded look came into Simon's eyes, which made her realise she shouldn't have known that. "Sorry, my friend again. She mentioned it."

"She knows quite a bit," Simon remarked. "What else did she say about me?" Olivia hesitated, feeling both guilty and trapped, and he shrugged. "It's okay. I figure there's something. At the start of the evening you were looking a little wary."

"Sorry." Olivia wished now more than ever that Harriet hadn't said anything to her. "She didn't say anything more, actually. Just that…" How to put it? "You're not a serial killer."

Simon let out a huff of laughter. "That must have been a great relief to you."

"Well, I wish she hadn't said anything. I'd rather learn about you from you."

"So if I'm not a serial killer, what did she think I am?"

"She didn't say," Olivia said wretchedly. She could tell, despite Simon's easy manner, that he was hurt, and she hated that. "Just that there had been rumours…of something." As soon as she said the words, she regretted them. They sounded *awful*.

"Ah." His gaze had turned distant, and Olivia waited, wondering if he was going to explain. If she wanted him to. "Well, like you said, you should learn about me from me."

"Yes…"

"And hopefully you've liked what you've learned so far."

"Yes, I have. I really have." He nodded slowly, and she

realised he wasn't going to tell her anything more, and she didn't know whether to feel disappointed or relieved. Whatever it was, it wasn't first date material, and she decided she was okay with that. No one wanted to air all their dirty laundry and deep secrets right away. It wouldn't be fair on either of them if he did. She felt better somehow, even though she knew she still didn't know anything—or at least not much.

"So." He smiled, his eyes crinkling, his tone and expression deliberately light. "What do we talk about now?"

"Sorry that was all a bit of a buzzkill, wasn't it?" She grimaced. "How do you like Wychwood-on-Lea?"

"I like it. It's quiet, peaceful. And as it happens, your friend doesn't have up-to-date information. I'm about to move out of my sister's right after Christmas."

"Oh? Where to?"

"A converted stables cottage in the grounds of the local manor."

"Willoughby Close?" Olivia answered in surprised delight. "You must be moving into number three or four."

"Yes, that's right, number four." He cocked his head. "You know it?"

"Yes, my good friends live there. In numbers one and two, although they're both moving on soon."

"So the place will be empty save for me?"

"Yes, I suppose at first…but the other cottages are sure to be let soon."

"Something to look forward to, then."

"Yes, if you like neighbours."

"My neighbours in London kept to themselves. It's one thing I like about living in a village. People care."

"And they gossip."

"So I've noticed." He kept his voice light and Olivia smiled, glad he could joke about it.

"Anyway, Willoughby Close is lovely. I'd live there myself if I didn't have the flat."

The pub, Olivia noticed, had started to empty out. It was getting late and she had an early start tomorrow, as usual…yet she felt reluctant for the evening to end. "I suppose I should get going," she finally said. "Five a.m. wakeup to bake three cakes, scones and muffins, and of course, some cupcakes."

"What flavour tomorrow?"

"Nutella. Today was raspberry cheesecake. You didn't come for your cupcake." She meant to sound teasing but a faintly accusing note entered her voice.

"I'm sorry, I was stuck at school sorting out some paperwork for music exams. And…" he gave a sheepish grin "…I knew I'd be seeing you later anyway."

"Are you saying you've only been coming into the shop to see me?" Olivia dared to ask, her cheeks warming at the thought.

"Well, I must admit it's not for the cupcakes."

"What!" She pretended to look outraged.

"They're delicious, I'm sure, but I haven't eaten any." He paused, hanging his head. "The truth is, I didn't come into the shop for the cupcakes, or any of your other delectable treats. I came in to see you."

"Oh…" She was flummoxed and pleased by this admission, and she didn't know how to respond.

Simon cocked his head, his gaze thoughtful. "I saw you through the window and thought, she looks like someone I'd like to know."

Olivia's cheeks warmed as she stared at his honest, open face. "Oh," she said again.

"Is that creepy?"

"No, no…it's…it's sweet." It was rather wonderful. She laughed, willing her blush to fade, absurdly touched by his admission. "Thank you."

"Shall I walk you back to the shop?"

"All right."

Simon settled their bill, gallantly refusing Olivia's offer to split it, and then they stepped out of the pub into the cold night, their breath creating frosty puffs of air.

The high street of Wychwood-on-Lea was spangled with fairy lights and empty of people as they walked slowly down the cobbled pavement, the stars twinkling high above, diamond pinpricks in a dark night sky.

As the blue-painted door of Tea on the Lea came nearer, Olivia wondered what would happen. Should she invite him in? It was quite late now and she didn't want him to get ideas, but neither did she want the evening to end.

With each step she wondered how to handle that ever-awkward moment, the goodbye on the first date. Kiss his cheek? Shake his hand? Do the cringe-worthy hug?

"Do you want your cupcake?" she blurted as they both came to a halt outside the shop. "I saved one for you."

"Did you? That was kind. And most certainly worth five pounds."

She laughed as she unlocked the door and stepped inside. "I raised the price to three pounds, actually. I think that's reasonable."

"Eminently so."

She fumbled with the lights, her heart starting to thud in both expectation and nerves. "Well, you should take the cupcake anyway. I certainly don't want to eat it. I've been eating far too many as it is."

Simon stood by the door while Olivia fetched the cupcake, putting it in a box as she always did. Her fingers felt thick and clumsy, and she knew her face was scarlet. She was nearly *forty*, for heaven's sake. Far too old for these kinds of jitters.

"May I see you again?" Simon asked. "This weekend?"

"Yes, I'd like that. I'm working Saturday, but..."

"How about Sunday? We could go ice-skating. Apparently there's a pond on the other side of the Lea that's frozen over."

"Ice-skating..." That was novel. "I don't have any

skates..."

"I'll come prepared."

Olivia gazed at him; his eyes were warm and full of kindness, his smile wry, his hair flopping across his forehead. She didn't care what Harriet had said. She liked him...and she definitely wanted to see him again, even if it meant making a fool of herself and falling flat on her back on the ice.

"I'm not a very good skater."

"Neither am I. We'll have to hold on to each other, to keep us both up."

She liked the sound of that. She liked the sound of it all. "All right. I see my mum in the late morning but I could meet you after that."

"Shall I pick you up from here?"

"All right. Thank you." She handed him the box, his fingers sliding over hers as he took it. "Your cupcake, sir."

"Many thanks, my lady." He grinned and then stepped back, which gave her a little flicker of disappointment. So he wasn't even going to try to kiss her. "I'll see you Sunday."

"Yes. Sunday." He gave a mock salute and then left, the jingle bells on the door ringing merrily as he shut it behind him. Olivia let out a gusty sigh as she locked up and turned off the lights. She'd been hoping the evening would have ended a little differently, even if it had just been a kiss on the cheek. Still, she told herself as she headed upstairs, she had Sunday to look forward to.

Chapter Nine

"SO HOW WAS it?"

Alice's eyes were alight as she came into Tea on the Lea the next day, intending to buy six Nutella cupcakes for a dinner she and Henry were having. She'd barely got through the door, however, before blurting out her question.

Olivia raised her eyebrows, determined to play cool. "How was what?"

"Your date." Alice dropped her voice to a theatrical whisper even though there was no one else in the shop; Evelyn Dearborn, a lovely old lady, had just had her morning tea and scone and had left as Alice came in, but she was mostly deaf anyway.

"I gather you've been talking to Harriet?"

"Yes, sorry." Alice gave a guilty smile. "Should she not have said?"

"No, it's fine." Judging from Alice's unbridled enthusiasm, Harriet hadn't mentioned the so-called rumours about Simon, for which Olivia was grateful. "And the date was good. Really good. We're seeing each other again on Sunday."

"Oh, Olivia!" Alice clasped her hands together. "I'm so pleased. Is he nice?"

"He is," Olivia said firmly. There was absolutely no doubt about that. Simon Blacklock was the nicest man she'd ever met. And she still wished he'd kissed her last night.

"Oh, that sounds lovely. What are you doing on Sunday, then?"

"We're going ice-skating at that pond on the other side of the Lea." Olivia couldn't stop herself from making a bit of a face. It had sounded fun and Christmassy last night, but now she was realising how little ice-skating experience she had, i.e. nil, and how likely she was to make a complete fool of herself.

"How romantic," Alice gushed. "Skating around hand in hand…I love it."

"Or falling flat on my face. I've never been ice-skating before."

"Me neither," Alice said. Growing up as a lost cause in the foster system, there was a lot Alice hadn't done, Olivia knew—and too much that she'd had to. "But it does sound nice. And if Simon is so nice, he's hardly going to laugh at you or something for falling over."

"I know, but…it's all very new." And fragile. And that made her scared. Last night she'd lain in bed reliving the best parts of her evening with Simon, and then remembering the awkwardness of her confession—and Simon's lack of one.

She knew she was already starting to care about him—that was a freight train of feeling she had no control over, it seemed—but she also knew that when you cared you got hurt. Her lack of romantic relationships was a testament not just to her inability to find a Mr Right, but also a deliberate choice not to put herself out there. It simply wasn't worth it.

But could it be now? Could Simon be worth it? Of course she didn't have enough information to answer that question yet, but already her emotions were galloping ahead of her far more rational thoughts.

"Relationships are scary," Alice commiserated with a sympathetic smile. "Not that I have loads of experience. Henry was my only boyfriend, the only man I ever kissed, even."

"Do you wish there had been others?" Olivia asked. She'd had a few boyfriends over the years, and definitely kissed a few frogs, but she still felt inexperienced and uncertain now, in light of this. Of Simon.

"No, I don't," Alice answered. "Because I found Henry. I admit, sometimes I feel gauche compared to him or, well, anyone, but I'd rather be gauche than jaded. Naïve rather than cynical."

"That's the right attitude, Alice. Definitely better to live your life on the side of hope." Which was sort of what she was doing, even if a part of her kept holding back as well as on to that ever-persistent fear. She didn't want to be cynical about Simon, even her wary, rational side warned her that he was almost certainly too good to be true, whatever Harriet had or hadn't said.

"Are you coming to the mulled wine and mince pies evening?" Olivia asked as she boxed up the cupcakes. "Although I think I should come up with a catchier name."

"I wouldn't miss it for the world," Alice answered. "And I've invited a few people that Henry knows."

"Thanks, Alice. I'm hoping to get a good crowd."

"And so you should. It sounds like loads of fun."

Olivia hoped so. Sometimes she wondered if the special events she offered were overlapping with similar offerings from the school, church, or village hall, but she had to keep trying, and she liked planning them. Harriet had already designed a poster to put up throughout the village.

Olivia spent the rest of the weekend, all the way up to Sunday afternoon, trying to keep herself busy and not obsess about Simon. She made a sign announcing the mulled wine and mince pies evening and propped it in the shop window, and even got a few enquiries about it.

She made three batches of shortbread and planned her next few flavours of cupcake, and during a slow moment in the shop she did some Internet shopping for her Christmas presents. She debated whether to get Simon a present and then decided it was too much, too soon. She wouldn't even know what to get him, anyway.

Late Sunday morning she drove to Witney to visit her mum; she'd called every day to check in, but she still felt a bit anxious, and wondered if she should talk to one of the managers of her mother's building. The retirement community was built so its residents could hold on to as much independence as possible, and at the moment Tina was living completely free of any interference.

Olivia was reluctant to change that, but what if it was necessary? Her mother had already burned herself at least twice. The last thing Olivia wanted to do was compromise her well-being—what if she needed the next level of care, someone to check in on her, a carer of some sort? Olivia instinctively dismissed the idea; her mum was her mum, matter-of-fact and completely capable…except somehow she wasn't, anymore.

When she arrived at her mother's flat, however, Tina was looking remarkably well put together and seemed happier and more alert than she had been in a while. She'd even put up some Christmas decorations—the old nativity set was in pride of place on the hall table.

"You decorated," Olivia said with a delighted smile. She felt inordinately happy that her mum had made the effort.

"I thought I ought to do something," Tina answered. "Even if it's something small. Now how are you?"

"Good. I went on a date last night, actually." She hadn't told her mum about Simon yet, and she hoped it wasn't too early to now.

"A date!" Tina smiled and clapped her hands together lightly. "Olivia, I'm so pleased. Who is this special man?"

"Simon Blacklock. He was the one who drove us to the hospital?"

"Oh yes." Her mother's brow crinkled, and Olivia couldn't tell if she really remembered him or not. "How lovely. Was it nice? Where did you go?"

"Yes, it was. Very nice. We went out for a drink at the pub, and we're going ice-skating later today."

"So it sounds like it could be serious?" Tina's eyes twinkled, making her look years younger.

"It's too early to say," Olivia said quickly. "We're just getting to know one another. Anyway." She moved into the kitchen, deciding it was time to change the subject. "Enough about me. How are you?"

"I'm well, all things considered." Tina followed her into the kitchen and filled the kettle. "In some ways, it's almost a relief," she explained as she carefully put the kettle on the stove, watching the open flame.

"What's a relief, Mum?"

"The diagnosis."

"You haven't actually—"

"It's coming, Olivia. You know that. Whether it's now or the appointment after Christmas, or another test or scan after that. It's coming. And it's a relief."

Olivia struggled to keep hold of her feelings as well as her expression. How could it possibly be a *relief?* She didn't want to ask the question, yet her mother must have seen it in her face.

"I know it must be difficult for you to understand," she said gently as she handed Olivia a cup of tea just as she liked it, milky and sweet. "But for so long I've been denying what was going on, even to myself. Especially to myself. I explained away a thousand little things because I didn't want it to be true. I didn't want to lose myself."

"And now?" Olivia asked, struggling to keep her voice level. She felt as if she could burst into tears.

"Now I am starting to face that fear, and strangely, it's not as overwhelmingly horrible as I thought." She smiled at Olivia as she sipped her tea. "It's still frightening, and of course I'd rather it wasn't happening, but besides all that I'm okay. At least now I don't have to pretend I have it all together."

"I wish you'd never pretended, Mum. If I'd known, I could have helped…"

"Pretending was an instinct. But it made me even more anxious, always trying to cover how lost I felt, and I'm sorry for that. I know I haven't seen myself these last few months, and now, bizarrely, I feel more like myself. Even if I can't remember how to draw a clock." Tina's lips trembled and Olivia's heart ached. No matter how brave or pragmatic her mother was being now, this was still hard. It was terrifying.

"How long had you been pretending?" she asked. "Do you reckon?"

Tina pursed her lips as she sat back in her seat. "I don't know. Longer, perhaps, than I even realise now. Too long."

"When you asked me to come back and help out at the shop…" Tina nodded and Olivia swallowed hard. That had been nearly two *years* ago. "Well, the important thing now is to look to the future," Olivia said as briskly as she could. "I've done a little research online, Mum, and there are ways to boost your memory and stave off the worst of the symptoms. That is," she added hurriedly, "if you even—"

"Olivia," Tina cut her off gently. "I do."

"Well, still. It's not the end of the world. People can live with—with dementia for a long time." But it had already been two years.

"I know that, and I'm glad you do, as well. It's not the end, Olivia. In some ways, it's just the beginning."

But the beginning of what? As much as Olivia wanted to hold on to the hope of medical research and the amazing benefits of ginkgo biloba, she knew her mother could only stave off the symptoms for so long. Decline was eventual, inevitable…but then she supposed that was true for everyone.

"I know," she managed, trying to smile for her mum's sake. "I'm just taking time to get used to this." Olivia smiled wryly. "You seem to be handling it much better than I am."

"You'll get there. It's more of a shock to you than it was to me."

Olivia finished her tea, reluctant to leave her mum, but time was getting on. "I suppose I should go," she said. "I'm meeting Simon in less than an hour."

Her mother smiled, her eyebrows raised expectantly. "Simon? Who's Simon?"

BACK AT TEA on the Lea, Olivia headed upstairs to change into warmer clothes. It was a perfect day for enjoying the wintry weather—crisp and cold with blue skies and bright, hard sunshine that made every blade of grass sparkle with frost.

Dr Jekyll prowled around her as she squeezed herself into some thermals, wincing at her reflection before she hurriedly put on the rest of her clothes. She'd just yanked on a pair of sturdy boots when she heard a tapping on the glass downstairs.

Dr Jekyll trotted behind her, wanting to investigate, and then decided to be extra-friendly by jumping into Simon's arms as Olivia opened the door.

"Oh, hello there!" he exclaimed as he caught the cat instinctively. "So you're being friendly today."

"For the moment," Olivia answered as Simon set him down on the floor. "Be careful of his claws."

"Wise advice." Simon straightened, brushing his inky hair away from his eyes as he gave her one of his wry smiles. He had a large bag thrown over his shoulder, which Olivia assumed held their skates. "Are you ready?"

"Yes, I'll just get my coat."

"Do you mind walking?" Simon asked as they set off

down the high street, the air cold enough to sting Olivia's cheeks. "It's not that far, and there isn't much parking there, or so I've heard."

"No, I don't mind at all. It's a beautiful day."

And it was beautiful, as they took the footpath at the top of the high street, pausing as they crossed the little wooden footbridge that spanned the Lea River, and offered a choc-late-box view of the village.

"You do know where this pond is, don't you?" Olivia asked, half-joking, as Simon strode down a narrow path that wound between a cluster of oak trees, their branches stark and bare now in the depths of December.

"More or less..." He glanced back at her with a cheeky smile that made her laugh. "Perhaps a little more less."

They walked along the footpath for another ten minutes, wending their way through a forest and then a tufty sheep pasture before Simon slowed and gestured with one arm. "Voila!"

Olivia stopped to gaze at the small pond, its surface smooth and gleaming ice. A handful of people were skating on it—a couple of kids who flung out their arms and stumbled along, and one woman who was doing sharp figure eights, a look of serene concentration on her face.

"Wow. I never even knew this was here. How did you hear about it?"

"My sister told me. She took my nephews here last week." He gestured to a fallen log someone had fashioned into a bench, sawing off the top so it was flat enough to sit on. "I borrowed her skates for you… I think you're about the same size."

"Six?" Olivia asked hopefully and he squinted as he glanced at the size printed on the inside flap.

"Seven. But you're wearing thick socks."

They suited up, Olivia's fingers feeling thick and clumsy as she laced her skates. "I think you should know," she warned him as they both stood and started to clump over towards the ice, "that I've never actually skated before, and I'm generally not the most dextrous person."

"I think you should know," Simon answered, "that neither am I."

In fact, as Simon gingerly stepped out on the ice, Olivia couldn't help but think how much he resembled a stork. A charming, handsome stork, but there could be no denying that his gangly frame was not the most graceful as he took a few exploratory glides along the ice, wobbling so much Olivia caught her breath in a would-be gasp, before Simon turned to her with a flourish, spreading his arms out wide.

"See? Easy," he said, and then promptly fell flat on his back.

"Oh!" Olivia half-skated, half-minced her way over to him, conscious of her own lack of balance, her flailing arms. "Simon, are you okay? Are you hurt?"

"Only my pride, and I have little enough of that as it is." He blinked up at her, grinning, and she gave a little laugh as she stretched out a hand to help him up. Simon took it, and for the next few seconds they were engaged in an awkward, imbalanced dance as they both struggled to right themselves and Olivia feared they'd end up crashing to the ground.

Simon grabbed hold of her forearm, and then steadied himself by putting his other hand on her waist, so it almost felt as if they were waltzing—admittedly rather badly. But still they were close, close enough that Olivia could see the silvery glint in his eyes, feel the heat of his body, and her heart rate skittered in response. They remained that way for a long, suspended moment, their faces and bodies both close, and then Simon steadied himself and, still holding her hand, started to skate.

Olivia had no choice but to keep up with him, trying to match his gliding strides, terribly conscious not just of his nearness but of how precarious her own balance felt. Around them a couple of kids were half-stumbling across the ice, and the lone woman did an impressive jump, spinning in the air before she landed neatly and skated on.

"I'm feeling a bit outclassed," Olivia murmured, and Simon shot her a quick smile.

"You shouldn't. I think you're doing just fine." He squeezed her hand and she tried to keep her heart—and hopes—from soaring at this little exchange. As much as she liked Simon, as much as she wanted this to work, she still felt instinctively cautious.

They managed three loops of the pond before Simon

suggested they take a break. The other skaters had left, and they had the pond to themselves, the air still and crystalline, the sun high in the sky.

They sat on the fallen log and Simon produced a flask of hot chocolate from his bag. "Sustenance," he declared, and rummaged again to brandish two plastic mugs.

"This is wonderful, Simon, thank you." Olivia took her cup of hot chocolate, savouring its sweetness.

"It was a challenge to come up with a second date activity," Simon told her with a grin. "If we'd gone to the cinema we couldn't have talked, and I'm not really good with parties, so that was out…"

"You're not good with parties?" Olivia said in surprise. "I would have thought you'd be the life of the party."

"Nope, I'm not really good with crowds." He glanced down at his mug, and Olivia felt that now-familiar frisson of wary curiosity as she wondered what he wasn't saying.

"So will you have Christmas with your sister and her family?" she asked, and Simon gave a little grimace.

"She's invited me, but they're all going to my brother-in-law's parents' and I'd feel like a fifth wheel. I barely know them."

"So what will you do then?"

Simon shrugged. "I'm getting the key to Willoughby Close just before Christmas Eve, so I might just spend the holiday moving in."

"That's no way to spend Christmas." Olivia hesitated,

wondering if it would be far too soon to ask him to spend Christmas with her. She decided it would, and so instead she invited him to the mulled wine and mince pie evening she had planned at the shop. "It's on Wednesday, and I'm hoping to get a crowd. There will be a bit of a carol singa-long, and then a Christmas quiz. Do you think you'd like to come?"

"I'd love to," Simon said, with such sincere enthusiasm that Olivia couldn't keep from breaking out in a grin of pure happiness.

"Good." Maybe this felt too good to be true…but maybe it was just *good*. She wanted to believe that. She chose to.

By the time they finished their hot chocolate and made another couple of circuits of the pond, dusk was starting to fall, creating pools of violet shadow among the trees.

"I suppose we should get back," Olivia said, even though she was reluctant to end their date. They had been holding hands as they skated along and even though her toes were numb and her cheeks felt raw she didn't want to leave.

"Yes, I can't feel most of my feet. But you didn't fall once, unlike me."

"I also skated at a snail's pace." They sat on the bench together and unlaced their skates, and then as they started back along the twilit path, Simon reached for her hand. It felt completely natural and right to walk along holding hands, and even though the path was a little too narrow to walk alongside each other, they somehow managed it.

Olivia's steps slowed as they came down the high street towards Tea on the Lea. Should she invite him in? Once again she was in a quandary, and then she decided she didn't need to be. Why worry so much? Why not simply take life's opportunities as they presented themselves? Find happiness and perhaps even love where and when she could?

She turned to him, so abruptly she nearly crashed into him. "Do you want to come in?" she asked a little breathlessly. "Have some dinner? I think I could rustle up something, or we could get a takeaway, although admittedly Wychwood doesn't have that many options. Fish and chips…"

"I'd love to," Simon answered, and Olivia's breath came out in a rush of relief. Maybe this really could be easy. Maybe it could be good. And she could stop being afraid, stop worrying about the what-ifs or the things she didn't know, and let everything unfold naturally…wonderfully.

Chapter Ten

O F COURSE, AS soon as Simon followed her upstairs, Olivia realised she had not left her poky little flat in a state to receive visitors. The kitchen was a mess of dirty dishes, an open box of cereal trailing its flakes across the counter, and her washing was hanging to dry on a rack in the middle of the sitting room, her rather worn M&S bras and pants on glaring display.

"Sorry, I wasn't expecting..." she began in a half-mumble before whisking the rack into her just-as-messy bedroom. She returned with an apologetic smile, and Simon laughed.

"You should see the state of my room."

"Will you be glad to get your own place?" Olivia asked as she hunted through the kitchen for something to offer. She should have done a weekly shop today, but between her mum and ice-skating with Simon she hadn't had the time.

"Yes, I think so," Simon said after a second's hesitation. "It will be nice to have some space."

"You must get along with your sister rather well if you're

able to live with her," Olivia remarked. She had a packet of pasta and a jar of sauce. Not the most inspired meal, and she realised belatedly that the fish and chip shop in the village was closed on Sundays.

"Yes, we do, mostly. I suppose any siblings fight."

"I wouldn't know, but that sounds right."

"Did you ever wish you had siblings?" Simon asked as he leaned against a kitchen counter, his long legs stretched out in front of him.

"Not really, actually. Mum and me always felt like a complete unit."

"How is she? You saw her this morning?"

"Yes, and she was surprisingly okay. But I'm still bracing myself for whatever lies ahead... It feels so unknown." Cue the wretched lump in her throat, the feeling that she was at sea, trying to keep her balance on a ship whose deck kept pitching and rolling with the waves of uncertainty.

"It must be hard," Simon said quietly, and she was grateful he didn't try to slap a "look on the bright side" plaster on what felt, at the moment, like a gaping emotional wound.

"Yes, it is, and will be. But at least Mum seems in a good place emotionally." Olivia thought of how serene her mother had seemed this morning, and then how she'd completely forgotten any mention of Simon. That had jarred Olivia, the obvious lapse, one her mother wasn't even aware of. How many more would there be? And how had she not seen them before?

"So, dinner," Olivia said brightly. "Would you like some spaghetti with a jar of sauce? Sorry it's not more inspired."

"Your cupcakes are inspired."

"And yet you haven't tried one."

"I will, I promise." His eyes glinted at her, a smile quirking the corners of his mouth. "And yes, I'd love pasta and sauce. But why don't you let me cook? You do enough work in the kitchen as it is."

"Oh…" Olivia felt jolted. A man cook for her in her own kitchen? It was a strange and yet surprisingly pleasing thought.

"That is, if you don't mind me moving around your space, using your stuff," Simon said with a grin.

"No, I don't. I can't remember the last time someone cooked for me." She took a seat at the tiny kitchen table while Simon began hunting around for pots and pans, finding them with alacrity.

It was wonderfully companionable, to chat about nothing important while Simon put a pot of water on to boil, and found some garlic and mushrooms to add to the sauce, chopping everything with brisk precision.

"You seem like you know your way around a kitchen," Olivia remarked. He'd also found a bottle of wine and asked if he could open it; now they were both sipping from glasses of red while Simon continued with his preparations.

"I suppose I do, a bit. I've lived on my own for most of my adult life, and awhile ago I got tired of takeaways and noodles in a mug."

"I'm ashamed to admit I cannot say the same."

"You do enough in the kitchen, with all your baking. I can certainly understand why you'd be reluctant to make a big meal at the end of the day."

"I suppose I couldn't see the point, when it was just for me."

"True. I got over that by having people around for a meal as often as I could. I'm better with people around me."

"So you're not an introvert?" Olivia teased.

"Oh, I am, undoubtedly, too much so. I need people to bring me out of myself."

"Hmm." She took a sip of wine, mulling that over. "I wouldn't have thought you were an introvert. You seem so...sociable, I suppose. Friendly and interested in everything."

"I try to be. Life is short. I want to enjoy as much of it as I can." A bleak note had entered his voice, making Olivia wonder.

"That's true enough," she said after a moment. "And a good motto to live by."

"I try. I don't always succeed."

"I don't suppose anyone does." This had all become rather deep, but she didn't mind. She was enjoying simply sitting in her own kitchen, watching Simon cook. His long, lean fingers flew dextrously as he chopped vegetables and then sautéed them in a pan, the mouth-watering aromas of garlic and mushrooms soon wafting through the air and filling the space.

Outside night had fallen like a velvet curtain, pierced only by the twinkle of the fairy lights that spangled the high street. Even Dr Jekyll was contributing to the feel-good factor, twining about Olivia's legs before leaping into her lap and settling there with a loud, rattling purr. She stroked his fur and sipped her wine, nearly completely content. Like Simon had just said, she wanted to enjoy this moment for what it was, without looking back or wishing for more. Olivia leaned her head back and closed her eyes, revelling in the easy pleasure of simply being.

"Here. Try this."

She opened her eyes, startled, to see Simon placing a small plate of bruschetta in front of her, heaped with chopped tomatoes and flecked with basil.

"When did you make this!" Olivia exclaimed. "I didn't even notice…"

"You had some leftover baguette that was going stale. It was easy."

"And delicious." She took a bite, enjoying the explosion of flavour. This man was a keeper. He could cook, he was kind and funny and thoughtful, and she was, Olivia could not deny, rather desperately attracted to him. She hoped he felt the same, but sometimes Simon could be so hard to read.

As she took another bite of bruschetta she watched him stir the pasta, his tall, lanky form somehow seeming right in her tiny kitchen. His jumper, she noticed, had holes in the elbows and was coming unravelled at the hem. His jeans were faded, his hair still a little long, and he'd taken off his boots and was wearing mismatched socks. He looked a little bit like a hobo—a handsome, lovable hobo, because Simon's quirkiness was all part of his undeniable appeal.

But what was her appeal? What did he see in her? Olivia knew she could stand to lose ten pounds or even a stone, her hair went frizzy at the least provocation, and while she could bake a host of goodies, so far Simon didn't seem to particularly like cupcakes. She was kind enough, she supposed, and she had a decent sense of humour, but really…what might Simon see in her?

Why was she even doing this? Romance wasn't a pros and cons list, surely. You didn't tot up all your good qualities and hope they were enough to make the grade. But what was it then? It amazed Olivia that at her age she still needed to ask this question; she hadn't figured out the answer. What made a person worth the risk? What made you fall in love?

"What are you thinking about?" Simon asked, glancing over his shoulder as he drained the pasta. "You have a very serious look on your face."

"Do I?" Olivia was not about to admit she'd been thinking about love. "Just…this and that, really." And then she blushed, which gave the game away.

"And what was this?" Simon asked with a teasing smile. "Or that?"

"Oh…" She could feel her face going positively scarlet, which was really not a good look for her. She had a comfortably round face to match her figure and when she flushed she tended to look like a tomato. "Well, if you want to know the truth," she said recklessly, her heart pounding at the thought of her daring, "I was thinking about romance."

Simon's eyebrows rose as he put two plates of pasta on the table and then sat down opposite her. "That sounds intriguing."

"I just wondered what made a person fancy another. Or fall in love, for that matter." Had she gone too far? Time to get this conversation under control. "You mentioned you were engaged a while back. What made you fall in love with your fiancée?"

"I don't know if I could pinpoint it exactly," Simon answered after a moment. "We had fun together, we liked the same things, we shared the same values. Or I thought we did, until she moved on." He shrugged. "Can you boil it down to a formula or an equation? I suppose scientists and philosophers have been trying to figure that one out for eons."

"Yes, I suppose they have." Olivia thought of Rob, her most serious boyfriend from a decade ago. What had made them a good couple, if they even *had* been a good couple? She wasn't sure anymore that they had been; she had been the one to cool things off, at any rate, because she hadn't been able to see a long-term future together. Rob had been nice enough, but he'd been ambitious and impatient about it, and Olivia had known she wouldn't fit into his lifestyle in the long run.

"I think it's more of a feeling rather than a formula," Simon said, his chin propped in her hand. "One of rightness, that this fits, that you can be yourself, your true self, with a person. You can't pinpoint why, although I suppose sometimes you can pinpoint why not."

"Yes…" Olivia half-wished she hadn't started this conversation. It felt like too much, too soon, but at her age, how long did she really want to wait to tackle the big stuff? "So, is it just you and your sister?" she asked in a rather obvious bid to change the subject. "Or do you have other siblings?"

Simon's alert, interested expression—the crinkled eyes, the ready smile, suddenly shut down. It was odd, like watching a curtain come down, something being wiped completely clean. He took a bite of pasta, chewed and swallowed before answering carefully, "It's just the two of us now. My younger brother died eighteen months ago."

"*Oh.*" She'd really put her foot in it, that much was obvious. "I'm so sorry, Simon." She hesitated, unsure whether to probe, yet it felt insensitive to simply change the subject. "I can't even imagine how hard that must be."

He nodded slowly. "Very hard. It's why I moved to Wychwood, actually."

"Is it…?" She gazed at him encouragingly, waiting for more. She'd never seen Simon look so bleak, his face drawn into stark, serious lines. It made her ache for him; she wanted to go around the table and put her arms around him, but their relationship wasn't there yet and in any case he seemed a bit distant, retreating into himself before her very eyes.

"You know your friend who had heard rumours about me?"

Olivia swallowed and nodded. Was he going to tell her whatever the dark secret that had been lurking in the shadows was? Did she want to hear it? "Yes, I remember."

"Of course you do." He gave a twisted smile. "I suppose I should have told you before. I know things have been swirling about, whispers in the school playground and so forth."

"Well, I'm never in the playground, but I know what you mean." She took a quick, steadying breath. "But, Simon, you don't have to tell me anything you don't want to. I mean…we're getting to know each other on our own terms, aren't we? That's enough for me."

"I'm glad we're getting to know each other, but this is part of it, isn't it? To tell the truth of who we are, where we've been." He propped his elbows on the table, giving her a direct, resolute look, the shadows still visible in his eyes. "It's not easy to talk about, and I fully admit I made a pretty big mistake." Now she was feeling really nervous. "But…after my brother died, I was in a bad place. He died in a rock climbing accident… We were climbing together, in Switzerland. Andrew was all about extreme sports, and he wanted to go climbing for his thirty-fifth birthday. I wasn't as into it, but I agreed." He paused, his gaze distant, and then released a long, low breath. "So we went, and we were rappelling…both of us on ropes with fixed anchors, right next to each other."

Olivia nearly shivered at his flatly delivered description, knowing what had to come next.

"His anchor came loose," Simon explained in that same, flat voice. "And for a few seconds he dangled there, knowing it was coming out and that he could fall hundreds of feet, most certainly to his death." He swallowed hard. "I was close enough to grab on to him, and I did. But my anchor couldn't hold both of us, and Andrew realised that. As I held him he let go. I watched him fall."

Tears rose to Olivia's eyes and she furiously blinked them back. "Oh, Simon, I can't even imagine how…" She couldn't continue; any sentiment seemed trite, falling far too short of the grief he'd experienced. "I'm so, so sorry."

Simon nodded, accepting. "It was the hardest and most horrible thing that has ever happened to me. And afterwards I had…" He paused, choosing his words with care. "I had trouble coping," he finally said. "I was teaching A level music at an independent school in London and the kids were so entitled, so ridiculously privileged without any sense of how much they had—the opportunities, the possibilities, life just stretching in front of them and they always acted so bored by it all, as if they couldn't even be bothered." He took a deep breath. "Anyway, I know of course that they had no bearing on my brother, two completely separate things. I knew that then, but it happened one day in one of my lessons that I...well, I sort of flipped, I suppose." He shook his head. "I lost my temper because some poor kid hadn't done his homework, wasn't even trying. He had a lot of raw talent that he just wasted, because he was so busy watching YouTube or Snapchatting or whatever it was that sucked all his time. And it made me so angry, because my brother had so much potential—only thirty-five, a criminal psychologist, doing amazing, important work." Simon managed a sad, wry smile that nearly broke Olivia's heart. "So when I saw this kid acting so indifferent, rolling his eyes, refusing to try, it flipped some switch in me and I completely lost my temper. Shouted, flipped a desk over, broke someone's violin."

Shock rippled through Olivia at this admission. She could understand it, of course she could, but it was still hard to take in—Simon, this gentle, sensitive, quirky man, displaying such a frightening loss of control when in a position of authority.

"I was dismissed immediately, of course, and thankfully no charges were brought against me. I even managed to keep my teaching certification, although I've got a black mark on my record. I had to take an anger management course and for the first few months here, there had to be another staff member in the music lessons with me, which I understand but I also know I'd never do something like that again. It was a one-off, something that broke inside me, but won't again." He sighed heavily and leaned back. "Anyway, word got around here, and I've noticed some parents in the playground giving me looks. I don't blame them, really. But I also know I'm completely trustworthy with the pupils in my care." He raked a hand through his hair, shaking his head. "So now you know."

"Oh, Simon." Olivia shook her head, still near tears. "Thank you for telling me."

"Does it change anything?" he asked starkly. "Between us?"

"No, of course not," she answered, and then wondered if she'd been too quick to reply. *Did* it change things, knowing Simon had this difficult past? People were complicated, Olivia knew that, of course, but Simon was particularly so. And being with someone like that—loving someone like that—meant getting tangled up in their grief, wrestling with their issues…and that was hard. But just because something was hard didn't mean it was not worth pursuing.

"It doesn't change anything," she said at last, because ultimately it didn't. She still liked him. Still wanted to find out more about him, spend time with him. It just meant he had a history, just like she did. Like everyone did.

"Good." Simon smiled and twirled a forkful of pasta. "Sorry to offload all that on you. I didn't want to say it before because it feels like too much to process when you're just starting to get to know someone. You don't want to offload all your baggage at the first opportunity."

"I understand."

"Perhaps I shouldn't have said anything tonight."

"No, I'm glad you did. After all, I offloaded on you, didn't I? About my mum."

"I didn't mind."

"And I don't either." She smiled at him, and he smiled back, and it felt as if they'd reached an agreement of some kind. They'd taken a big step forward, even if they hadn't said as much. This relationship was going somewhere.

The rest of the evening passed amicably; they chatted about inconsequential matters as they finished their dinner and then Simon lit a fire and Olivia poured them both brandies, which they savoured in front of the crackling flames.

"You haven't got a Christmas tree," Simon remarked. "With everything decorated so marvellously downstairs, I would have thought you might have had one up here."

"I haven't had time," Olivia answered. She was curled up on one end of the sofa, her feet tucked under her, and Simon was sprawled on the other, his long legs stretched out so if she put her feet down they'd touch his. Not that she'd been obsessing about that, or anything.

"Are you going to decorate?"

"I suppose. Mum is still insisting that she's going to have her Christmas dinner at the retirement community in Witney, and it seems pointless to do it if I'm on my own."

"She might come round, still."

"I hope so. We've spent every Christmas of my life together." She blinked rapidly, embarrassed at how quickly she seemed to come to tears. "Sorry…"

"You don't ever need to be sorry for feeling something, Olivia," Simon said quietly, his tone so heartfelt that he nearly set her off again.

"So what are you going to do for Christmas, really?" she asked as she dabbed at her eyes. "Surely not just moving in, like you said?"

"I think so."

"That's no way to spend Christmas." He shrugged, and Olivia took a deep breath. Should she…? And then—why not? "Why don't you spend Christmas with me?" she blurted.

Simon's eyebrows rose. "Do you mean that?"

"Yes…but only if you want to. If you'd rather be alone, I'll understand." Although she'd be a bit hurt.

"No, I wouldn't, it's just…" He hesitated, and Olivia bit her lip.

"What is it?"

Simon looked torn, his mouth turning down apologetically. "I'm not always good with the big holidays," he said at last. "Since…since Andrew died."

"Oh, Simon, of course." She should have realised it might be a hard time for him. "I understand that. But…but that's okay, isn't it? I mean we could still…" She trailed off, unsure where she was going.

"Yes, we still could," Simon said, smiling, and Olivia sat back against the sofa cushions with a feeling of relief—and excitement. Because he'd said it all, really, hadn't he?

Chapter Eleven

"THOSE LOOK AMAZING. Far too good to eat."

Olivia let out a laugh as she gazed at the platter of red velvet cupcakes, the buttercream icing whipped into silky swirls, decorated with holly leaves cut from royal icing and dusted with edible gold glitter.

"I think they might be my best yet." She placed one on top, holding her breath as she made sure they wouldn't come toppling down.

"Everything looks fab. How many people do you think will be coming?"

It was three o'clock on Wednesday afternoon, and Olivia's Christmas Carols & Quiz Evening—Harriet's suggestion to give it that name—was due to start in a couple of hours. She'd spent the whole week getting ready, from perfecting her mulled wine recipe (more cloves) to baking enormous amounts of shortbread, mince pies, and of course, cupcakes.

"I really don't know." She wiped her hands down the sides of her jeans, nerves fluttering in her tummy for all sorts of reasons. She'd put a lot into this evening, and she hoped it might put Tea on the Lea on the map for many villagers who had simply walked by it in the past. She would also be seeing Simon again; he'd come in for his cupcake for the last two days, but both visits had been quick, little more than a chat over the till as she gave him his change. She was looking forward to seeing him properly tonight; things had shifted between them since Sunday, had become both more intense and more comfortable, an intimacy growing between them that both thrilled and scared her when she thought about it, which she did pretty much constantly.

"So how are things with Simon?" Ellie asked. All four of her friends had texted her after her ice-skating date, but Olivia had been a bit reluctant to impart any details. She'd simply said she'd had a good time, and they would be seeing each other again.

"They're good, I think," she said now as she put the platter of cupcakes to the side and turned to stir the simmering mulled wine. She still needed to shower and change before driving to Witney to pick up her mum, and then coming back here to commence the festivities.

"You think?" Ellie prompted with a gentle smile. "Or you know?"

"Well, it's still very new."

"Of course…"

"And it's a bit…" Olivia hesitated "…complicated."

"Complicated how?"

"Just…" She struggled to voice the feelings she'd been

dealing with over the last few days. "It's been a long time since I've been in a serious relationship—not that this is serious, yet. But it could be, and since neither of us is getting any younger, it's kind of on the table from the beginning, you know? It feels like there's more at stake."

"Yes," Ellie answered slowly, "I can understand that. I felt a bit like that with Oliver, at the start. I had Abby to consider, and we were both from such different backgrounds..."

"I suppose it's always complicated, isn't it? I mean two people trying to make their lives work together... It's never easy."

"No, but this is the fun part, surely?" Ellie asked, concern crinkling her brow. "The getting-to-know-you part, that first rush of—of excitement?"

"Yes, that part's lovely." Although Simon still hadn't kissed her, at least not properly. They'd had another awkward few moments at the door on Sunday night, shifting from foot to foot while they smiled uncertainly at one another before Simon leaned in and kissed her—on the cheek. His lips had been cool and soft and Olivia had been tempted—very tempted—to turn her face so their mouths collided. But she hadn't, because Simon seemed determined to take things slow, at least in that regard, and she could respect that. She wasn't some teenager to be slave to her hormones, although sometimes she felt like one.

"So what's the not-easy part?" Ellie asked.

"I suppose I'm just a little scared," Olivia admitted. "I haven't had a lot of relationships. I haven't really seen the point."

"Why not?"

She shrugged, uncomfortable. "I never met someone who seemed worth the risk."

"Ah, the risk." Ellie nodded in understanding. "It's so hard to put yourself out there when you've been hurt before."

"But I haven't been hurt before, not really," Olivia protested. "I called off my most serious relationships, and the dates that petered out hardly scarred my soul." Ellie gave her a funny look, as if Olivia was missing something obvious. "What?"

"It's just…I would have thought…I mean your dad. His leaving. That surely left a mark on you?"

"My dad…" Olivia repeated, surprised. She never even thought about her dad. She never wondered about him, why he left, what he might be doing now. Her mum hadn't told her much, just that it hadn't worked out and they were better off, just the two of them. She'd been briskly practical about it all, and she'd shown Olivia a few photos of the man who had fathered her. There was one of the three of them at Christmas, sitting in front of a fireplace; another at Blackpool, the pewter-coloured sea stretching out behind them.

"He's a good man, Olivia, but he wasn't cut out to be a father. We're fine as we are, aren't we, love?" And Olivia had always assured her that they were.

"Olivia...?" Ellie prompted. "Sorry if I'm overstepping the mark. I just thought...that's kind of a big thing, isn't it? To have your dad walk out?"

"I suppose," Olivia said, even as part of her thought, yes, of course it is. A very big deal. Yet she'd never acted as if it was, never felt the need to work through issues of rejection or abandonment. "It must seem strange to you, but I've never really thought about it. I was always happy with Mum and me, and I couldn't even remember my father."

"Sorry, perhaps I shouldn't have brought it up..."

"No, it's okay. Something to think about, anyway." She smiled, or tried to, but she felt strange inside, like part of her had just developed a hairline crack that was surely getting wider and wider. "I'd better shower and change. I'm due to pick Mum up soon."

"What can I do down here?" Ellie still looked concerned and apologetic, as if she regretted bringing the whole father thing up.

"Just man the fort, really. Stir the wine on occasion. I'll be as quick as I can."

Upstairs in her flat, Olivia knew she should hurry to get ready, but some strange and persistent curiosity had her taking a stool to reach the high cupboard above her bed where her mum stored all sorts of things—boxes of jumbled ribbons and thread, old cords to various appliances and devices that no longer worked, and photo albums.

Olivia took out the oldest one, the one she hadn't looked at very much. Her mum hadn't been much of one for photo albums; instead she and Olivia had made a framed collage of photos for each year of her childhood. Tina had taken many of them to her flat in Witney, and a few were still left here. But the collages started after Olivia was two.

Now she perched on the edge of the bed and opened the dusty album, smoothing the wrinkled plastic that covered the old, now-faded photos. There weren't many—a dozen in all, if that. Olivia couldn't remember the last time she'd looked at them. She'd never been curious, which now seemed odd; but in her child's mind she'd drawn a very firm line across the past. Her life had begun at age two, when it was just her and Mum.

Except of course it hadn't. She squinted, peering at the slightly blurry photo of them at Blackpool. Her father had her sandy hair, although his was cut short and didn't look frizzy. In the photo he had her hoisted on his shoulders and she had her arms around his neck like a little, smiling-faced monkey.

What had happened? Why had she never really wanted to know? How could a man, a loving husband and father judging by admittedly just a handful of snaps, have walked away from it all? From his own child?

A lump was forming in her throat, a stone in her stomach. She felt heavy, burdened by a weight she hadn't even realised she'd been carrying all these years. She'd always been *fine* about her dad's leaving. It had never mattered, because Mum was enough. And in many ways her mum had been enough, but there was, Olivia realised, a dad-shaped hole in her life, and there always had been.

Dr Jekyll stalked into the room and jumped onto her bed, startling her out of her reverie. With a jolt Olivia realised nearly half an hour had passed. She closed the album and put it on her bedside table, to look at later. Right now she needed to focus on the present.

An hour and a half later she was throwing open the door of Tea on the Lea to a satisfyingly large crowd—well, at least a dozen people, but the little shop couldn't fit many more. Christmas carols played merrily, and the space was filled with festive smells, ringing with laughter, filled with friends, acquaintances, and a few smiling strangers besides. More than one person told Olivia they hadn't even realised Tea on the Lea had been on the high street—but they were sure to stop in now. Words to warm her heart, and hopefully increase her bank balance.

Tina was circulating with platters of cupcakes and mince pies, and Ellie was doling out the mulled wine and apple cider, served in Olivia's ever-growing collection of mismatched teacups.

After an hour, when many of the cakes had been scoffed and cups of wine or cider drunk, Olivia decided it was time to start the Christmas quiz. Simon still hadn't made an appearance, and she tried not to let that bother or worry her as she called everyone to attention and began to hand out pencils and sheets of paper for the quiz.

"You can work in teams… Phones away please!" She gave a look of semi-mock severity at Harriet's husband Richard, who had been thumbing buttons on his phone.

"You can't get good reception in here, anyway," he said good-naturedly, and Harriet poked him in the ribs.

"Or anywhere in the village. Let's do this the old-fashioned way. Set a good example for the kids." She rolled her eyes at Olivia. "He's always been competitive."

"You're a good match, then," Olivia teased. The sound of jingle bells as the door opened had her lifting her gaze and then her heart turning over as she saw Simon coming in— unwinding his scarf, smiling sheepishly, looking wonderful.

"You're just in time for the quiz," Ava called out with a devilish glint in her eyes. "Why don't you go on Olivia's team?"

"I don't have a team," Olivia protested. "I know all the answers."

"Even so," Ava said, grinning. "It seems fitting."

"Oh, really." Olivia turned away to hide her blush. Ava didn't need to be so obvious, but Simon was laughing and somehow Olivia didn't mind. In fact, she rather liked it—the good-natured teasing, the feeling that she was part of something.

"Sorry I'm late," Simon murmured as he joined her at the front. "Stroppy parent."

"These Cotswold mummies can be quite precious about their children sometimes."

"Indeed. Have I missed very much?"

"Just a few cups of mulled wine." Olivia cleared her throat. "All right now! Question number one…"

The quiz went swimmingly, with plenty of good-natured competitiveness and joshing, and a bottle of fairly decent plonk to the winning team. Afterwards Olivia topped up more glasses and served more cakes, before they ended the evening with a collection of carols to sing.

I'm happy, she realised with a jolt as she stood side by side with Simon, singing *Ding Dong Merrily on High. Happier than I've been in a long while.* She didn't think she'd been unhappy all these years on her own, but she definitely hadn't felt like this. And yes, she knew that first rush of excited infatuation would pass, but already she hoped it might be replaced by something far deeper and stronger.

And Simon hadn't even kissed her yet. But perhaps he would tonight. By nine o'clock everyone was trickling out, and Ellie and Alice offered to start the washing-up while Olivia took Tina, who was looking quite tired, back to Witney.

"Will you stay?" she asked Simon as she headed out with her mum. "We could have a sherry upstairs after…"

Simon's mouth turned down at the corners and he shook his head. "I'm sorry… That sounds delightful but I really should get back."

"Oh. Okay." Olivia tried not to show her startled hurt.

She'd been expecting Simon to say yes. She'd thought they were both hurtling towards something, and while saying no hardly meant a screeching halt, it sort of felt like one.

She had to get over this ridiculous insecurity, she told herself as she helped Tina into her car. The night was black and breath-takingly cold, and the stars looked very far away. So Simon needed to get back home. No big deal. She didn't need to feel so rejected, as if everything was suddenly cast in doubt.

"Simon seems like a nice man," Tina remarked as Olivia started the car and headed out of the village.

"He is, Mum."

"I'm glad you've found someone, darling, I really am."

"Well, it's early days yet."

"I know, but I feel better knowing you're not alone."

"Mum…"

"Sorry." Tina held up a hand. "I'm not trying to sound melodramatic." She leaned her head against the seat. "I had a lovely time tonight."

"I'm glad, Mum." Olivia hesitated. "Will you come to the flat for Christmas, then? Simon will be there too and it would be lovely to spend the day together. I don't like thinking of you having some institutionalised dinner by yourself…"

"It's not that bad," Tina said reprovingly. "And the people are quite nice. I went to a coffee and cake morning a few days ago."

"You did?" Olivia was both pleased and surprised. It was

the first event her mother had gone to at the retirement community.

"Yes, I did. I figured I needed to start meeting people, before I lose all my marbles."

"Oh, Mum—"

"I'm joking, Olivia." Tina smiled at her. "Sort of."

"I'd still like you to have Christmas with us," Olivia persisted. She didn't want to nag, but she worried her mum was insisting on staying in Witney out of some misplaced sense of not wanting to be a bother. "If you want to."

Tina turned to look out the window. The wolds were cloaked in darkness. "Wouldn't you rather spend it with your new man?"

"No, I'd rather spend it with you. Seriously, Mum." Olivia didn't want to sound macabre by saying something about who knew how many Christmases together they had left, but she felt it. She wanted to enjoy life as it came, just as Simon had said back in the pub. Take each moment and hold it in her hand. Savour what—and when—she could.

"All right," Tina relented. "If you insist. I just don't want to be a bother."

"You won't be," Olivia promised. "At all."

Back at Tea on the Lea, after dropping her mother off, Olivia found the shop and kitchen both sparkling clean, with Ellie draping a damp tea towel over the oven railing, and Alice putting the last few cakes in Tupperware.

"You're too wonderful," Olivia said, hugging them both.

"I was expecting to have to be up for hours."

"Glad to be of service," Ellie said cheerfully. "It was a fab evening, Olivia. You deserve to put your feet up."

Which was what she'd wanted to do—with Simon. Olivia tried not to let that bother her as she headed upstairs to her flat, kicking off her low heels with a groan of relief. Dr Jekyll was in Mr Hyde mode, hissing at her from the corner of the kitchen, but Olivia just ignored him.

"You're warm and fed and cosy," she said as she collapsed onto the sofa. "You have nothing to complain about."

And neither did she. So Simon had declined her invitation. It wasn't a big deal. At least, it didn't have to be a big deal, if she chose not to make it one. She hugged her knees to her chest, willing herself to feel that, or at least to believe it.

A text pinged on her phone, and she snatched it, her heart lifting when she saw it was from Simon.

Sorry I didn't come round. I don't think I'd be very good company.

But he'd been charming company all evening. Frowning, Olivia deliberated over her response. *It's okay, Simon,* she finally texted. *Another time.*

She sent it, waiting for his reply, but none came. Tossing the phone aside, Olivia gazed into the empty fireplace, the ashes of their fire from the other day filling the grate, and she tried to decide if his text had made her feel better—or worse.

Chapter Twelve

AFTER THE SUCCESS of the Christmas Carols & Quiz Evening, Olivia decided to give herself a break and close the shop for the week of Christmas. She wanted time to relax, to spend with Simon, and to focus on her mum—and she didn't usually get much custom during Christmas anyway, as everyone was busy at home with their families.

First, of course, she had to finish her cupcake promotion, which she did on the twentieth of December, with a big, red and green sign in the window advertising the free cupcake for "loyal customers." She made a batch of triple chocolate cupcakes and another of her own creation, Christmas cake cupcakes, complete with brandy-soaked fruit and marzipan icing, which she gave away for free.

Over twenty people, all told, came in to buy their last cupcake and get their card stamped, and Olivia decided the promotion had been more than worthwhile—she gave Mallory another six Nutella cupcakes, her favourite flavour, as a thank you for giving her the idea.

Simon came in as well, and even though Olivia had seen

him a few days ago, at the quiz night, her heart still did that squeezy thing that it seemed to do every time she caught sight of him.

He waited until the crowd had dissipated before asking her if she'd bought a Christmas tree yet.

"No, not yet. I've been a bit busy…"

"I was only asking because there is a Christmas tree farm nearby where you can cut your own tree down, and I thought it might be fun to go together." He smiled wryly, waiting for her reply.

"Oh, it would, but—" Olivia hesitated, imagining the massive firs and spruces that were undoubtedly farmed. "I'm thinking I'll need quite a small tree. More of a tabletop item."

"I'm sure they sell small ones," Simon said easily, and so they arranged to meet up the next day.

A few snowflakes were drifting down as Simon picked her up in his car, cheery as ever, and they fell into an easy camaraderie as they drove to the farm on the other side of Oxford.

"Do you have a saw?" Olivia asked somewhat dubiously. She'd never cut down her own Christmas tree before; she tended to buy them from the supermarket, prewrapped.

"Of course," Simon answered easily. "I borrowed it from my brother-in-law."

"When are they heading out for Christmas?"

"Tomorrow. And I pick up the keys for Willoughby

Close this afternoon."

"Oh!" Olivia was pleased for both Simon and the close itself, with a new resident to liven things up. "That's wonderful, Simon."

"When I've retrieved all of my furniture and things from storage, you must come over to dinner."

"I'd love that," Olivia answered, "but let me help you move in. That is, if you want me to…"

"That would be wonderful," Simon answered with a beaming smile, and Olivia grinned back. Everything suddenly felt so wonderfully simple—her, Simon, their fledgling relationship.

A short while later they arrived at the Christmas tree farm, and with guidelines given and saw in hand, they walked across a field glittering with frost to the selection of smaller trees one of the staff had directed them to.

"How about this one?" Olivia asked as they approached a small, squat tree. Simon shook his head definitively.

"Too stubby."

"Stubby?" Okay, actually, she could kind of see it. "Right, then. Do you see one you like?"

"Hmm." Simon rubbed his chin, looking around the field of trees with a connoisseur's discerning eye. "What about that one over there?"

Olivia looked where he pointed and then shook her head. "It's all bare on one side."

"All right, let's try again."

In the end, they decided they'd found the perfect, or almost, tree on the fifth attempt, and then spent a good twenty minutes taking turns sawing it. Lying flat on her back on the cold, frosty grass, staring up at the blue sky through a screen of pine needles as she sawed and sawed and her arm ached, Olivia couldn't remember feeling so happy.

"Are you getting tired? Let me have a go." Simon scooted next to her, and for a second his hip and leg were pressed to hers, his face so close if she turned her head they'd be kissing. Not that that was how she wanted their first kiss to happen.

Quickly Olivia scooted out from under the tree. No, she didn't want it to happen under a tree, but it *would* happen. Of that she was becoming more and more sure.

Once they'd managed to saw through the trunk, they lugged the tree back to the main barn, where attendants wrapped it up and helped to tie it on top of Simon's car. Then they repaired to the adjoining café for a much-needed hot chocolate, complete with whipped cream and marshmallows.

"This has been so fun," Olivia said impulsively as she plucked a pink marshmallow from the top of her hot chocolate and popped it into her mouth. "I'm so glad I closed the shop for the week. I haven't a holiday in ages."

"You weren't tempted to skip town and have a week in the sun somewhere?"

"By myself?" She made a face. "No, I'm glad to be in Wychwood, celebrating with my mum…and you."

She was really glad, more pleased perhaps than she wanted Simon to know. She'd tried to downplay the fact that they were spending Christmas together—her friends would make far too much of it—but it still filled her with both excitement and hope.

"So am I," Simon said, his smile and eyes both warm. Olivia smiled rather foolishly back. Really, everything felt just about perfect.

On the way back to Wychwood, Simon asked if she minded stopping by Willoughby Manor so he could pick up the keys for number four.

"No, of course not," Olivia said. "Who are you picking them up from?"

"The caretaker of the manor…Jace, I think his name is?"

"Yes, Jace. He's a good friend of mine. Well, his wife Ava is, especially. She used to live in number three."

It felt strange to pull up to the familiar courtyard of Willoughby Close with Simon; Harriet and Ellie had both already left for Christmas, and so the courtyard looked a little forlorn, the curtains drawn on all the windows except for number four. Olivia peeked inside and saw the empty sitting room where Alice's second-hand sofa had once resided.

"Do you know where Jace's cottage is?" Simon asked. "He said he lived nearby but I'm not sure he gave specific directions…"

"That sounds like Jace. It's through a little path on the

other side of the drive—I'll show you."

They walked through the wood bordering the drive, the branches bare above them, the well-worn path of packed dirt, now frozen hard. After a few minutes they emerged in a little clearing where Jace's caretaker cottage—a small, castle-like edifice—stood, complete with frilly gingerbread and a tiny turret.

"Wow," Simon said as he eyed the elf-like abode. "Not what I expected."

"No, it's a bit OTT, especially for a man like Jace."

They knocked on the door and a few seconds later Ava opened it, jiggling a fussy-looking William.

"Oh!" She stared at them both in surprise. "Hello, Olivia. And…Simon, isn't it?" They would never guess from Ava's innocent expression that she had asked Olivia for every last detail about the man in front of her.

"Yes, it is. I'm here for the key to number four…?"

"Oh, yes, of course. Olivia, would you mind…?" Before she could protest, Ava had thrust a fussing William into Olivia's arms.

"Oh…" Her arms closed around the warm, chubby baby as William gave her a direct and suspicious look. "Hello there." Inadvertently, perhaps instinctively, her gaze met Simon's and she smiled wryly, suddenly conscious of how…intimate this seemed, how suggestive. Simon smiled back, eyes glinting, and Olivia felt a happy, warm glow spread through her.

Then William started to howl.

"Oh…oh…come on now…" She jiggled an increasingly furious William, knowing nothing she did would do a bit of good. His face was screwed up and bright red, a trail of decidedly green snot snaking from his nose to his mouth. Ew.

"Sorry," Ava said, not sounding sorry at all. "He's getting his two front teeth and he's absolutely miserable."

"Right…" Olivia made to hand him back but Ava wasn't having it.

"So Simon, you're moving into number four? How wonderful. Jace will be here in a second with the key."

"Great."

"It will be nice to have someone in here, now that Ellie and Harriet are moving out," Ava continued, all innocence. "I've told Olivia she should rent one of these places. Get a little distance from the shop."

"Oh…?" Simon looked uncertain, and Olivia didn't know whether to feel outraged or amused. Ava had told her no such thing. What was she playing at?

"I'm happy where I am," she said firmly. "I couldn't afford the rent and of course it wouldn't be nearly as convenient."

"True, but studies have shown living at your place of work can have detrimental effects to—"

"I'm hardly living *in* the shop, am I?" Olivia cut across her. If Ava was trying to ferret out Simon's intentions, she wanted to stop her friend right now. She and Simon were managing just fine without kindly meant interference.

"Here's the key," Jace said cheerfully as he emerged from the back of the house. "Sorry for the wait, Simon."

"No worries, mate."

Olivia thrust a drooling William—he'd wiped his snotty face on her shoulder—at Ava, giving her as quelling a look as she could. Ava smiled back with unabashed innocence, cuddling William to her.

"Come on, little man. Let's get you cleaned up."

"Do you want me to walk over with you?" Jace asked. "I know you've seen the place before, but I can take you through it again if you like…"

"I think I'll be fine. I'll come back if I run into any problems."

"Cheers, then."

"We'll have to have you both over for supper when you've settled in, Simon," Ava called as she headed to the back of the house, William peering over her shoulder. "Do let us know when you've moved in."

"Sorry about that," Olivia said as they walked back to Willoughby Close.

"Sorry about what?"

"Ava…she means well, but…" Olivia trailed off, uncertain how to put it.

"Ava's fine," Simon said easily. "Cute baby, too."

"Yes." Olivia decided to drop the subject. If Simon was

fine with Ava's good-natured nosiness, then she could be, as well.

They came into Willoughby Close, and Olivia waited while Simon unlocked the door to number four. It opened with a creak, and he stepped aside so Olivia could go in first.

"So I gather you've been in here before?" he said as they both walked around the cosy living area, the galley kitchen in one corner, and a pair of French windows overlooking the tiny rectangle of frost-covered garden.

"It's an open-plan bedroom upstairs, with an en suite bathroom," Olivia said, and then, for no apparent reason, blushed. "Of course you've already seen it, sorry..."

"No, it's good. It's all good." Simon strolled towards the French windows and gazed out at the tiny garden. "It'll be good to have my own place again," he said, his tone reflective and a little bit sad.

"How long have you been living with your sister?"

"Four months." He paused, as if he was going to say more, but then he stayed silent and Olivia wasn't sure whether to prompt, press, or simply leave it be.

"This feels like a new beginning, doesn't it?" she said as she joined him at the window. The sun was starting to sink below the trees, sending its slanting rays across the garden, and gilding everything with a nimbus of gold.

Simon turned to her, and Olivia realised with a jolt how close he was. Close enough to see the glint of silver in his grey-green eyes, the faint stubble on his chin. Close enough to kiss.

"It really does," he said softly and Olivia held her breath, the moment spinning on, exquisite, endless, expectant.

His head dipped lower. She bit her lip, one hand clenching by her side as Simon's gaze turned hooded.

"Olivia..." he began, but she didn't have to answer because he was kissing her, his lips brushing softly against hers, the barest whisper, before settling more firmly. Olivia's eyes fluttered closed as sparks spread out from the touch of his mouth right down to her fingers and toes. She stood on her tiptoes as she wrapped her arms around his neck and returned the kiss with everything she had.

Everything about the moment was perfect, and like she'd just said, this was a new beginning—for both of them.

Chapter Thirteen

I<small>T WAS</small> C<small>HRISTMAS</small> Eve, and Olivia's flat was full of cosy, festive cheer. Olivia gazed around the little sitting room with the tree perched at an admittedly rakish angle on top of a table, decorated within an inch of its life by both her and Simon the day they'd brought it home from the Christmas tree farm. They'd both come down with a serious fit of the giggles as they'd draped the tree with every possible ornament, bauble, and garland that Olivia possessed, plus a few more fashioned by Simon from spare bits of ribbon and foil. It was OTT and garish and frankly wonderful.

That had been only four days ago, and yet in some ways it felt like a lifetime—a happy lifetime. Since she'd closed the shop and the primary school had broken up for the holiday, Olivia and Simon had been free to spend every moment together, and they just about had, revelling in each other's company in an entirely new and wonderful way.

After decorating the tree, Simon had stayed for dinner. Olivia had cooked this time: chicken marsala and angel hair pasta that they washed down with a bottle of red wine.

Then they'd watched a film on the telly, snuggled up on the sofa, and he'd finally left for home after a lingering good-night kiss in the darkened shop.

The next day they'd gone Christmas shopping in Oxford, strolling hand in hand down Cornmarket Street, rating the ornate window displays from one to ten, and then finishing with a leisurely, intimate dinner at the romantic No. 1 Ship Street, sharing a plate of plump oysters over candlelight.

Yesterday, on the twenty-third, Olivia had gone to see her mum, and Simon had half-jokingly invited himself along. He'd seemed surprised and pleased when Olivia had taken him at his word, though was concerned that he'd be infringing on her time with Tina; but her mum had been delighted and when Simon revealed that he knew how to play bridge, they'd spent several happy hours playing, taking turns with the fourth person's hand.

Olivia hadn't seen her mother looking so animated and lively in a long time, and although she had a few small memory blips, she still managed to come out ahead, finishing the afternoon with a magnificent three no trump bid.

"Your mum still seems sharp as a tack," Simon remarked as they headed back to Wychwood, after sharing a takeaway curry with Tina. Simon liked mushroom dopiaza, just as she did, which felt like another small but important sign of their serendipitous synchronicity.

"Sometimes she really does," Olivia agreed. "Other

times..." She sighed, looking out at the darkened blur of sheep pasture as Simon drove down the A40 towards home. "She has another, more involved cognitive test on the twenty-eighth, at a memory clinic in Witney. I'm both looking forward to it and dreading it, strangely."

"That's understandable."

"Is it?" Olivia shook her head. "If I could make this all go away, I would, in a heartbeat, but since I can't, I'm starting to feel a diagnosis might be a good thing. Mum certainly thinks so, although she's already made up her own mind about it, anyway."

"Diagnoses are good things," Simon said seriously. "Knowing what's wrong with you, being able to get the proper help and medication..." He hesitated. "That's really valuable." Olivia turned to gaze at him uncertainly; it seemed as if they weren't talking about her mum anymore.

"That's what Mum believes, anyway," she said after a moment. "It's the first, necessary step."

"Will you be okay...taking her to the appointment? I know it's not easy..."

"Yes, I think so." Olivia gave him a quick smile. "But I'd love to see you afterwards, if you don't mind me downloading everything onto you."

"Of course I don't." He reached over and squeezed her hand, and Olivia's heart expanded so it was hard to breathe, but in an entirely good way. How had they got here so quickly, so wonderfully? Her natural caution and innate fear kept creeping up but more and more she was pushing them firmly back and simply enjoying this time of getting to know each other. *Liking* each other.

She was tired of living life on the sidelines, the supporting role to everyone else's star. This was her story, her life. *Her love.*

Not, of course, that either of them had said those important words, but Olivia could envision saying them one day…perhaps even one day soon.

Now, alone in her cheerful and decorated flat, she checked the fish pie bubbling away in the oven—she and her mum had always had fish pie, as a tradition, on Christmas Eve. Olivia was going to pick Tina up from Witney, and then they'd head over to the Christmas Eve church service where Simon was playing, before all having dinner together. Tina would spend the night and Simon would return in the morning to spend Christmas with them. Really, it was all perfect.

A text pinged on her phone from Harriet. *How's it all going?*

That was quite restrained for Harriet, but Olivia had been sparing with the details. She'd told her friends Simon was spending Christmas with her and Tina, but that was all. She hadn't gone into all the other time they'd spent together, or how hard and fast she was falling for him. She wasn't ready to share those things, didn't want them exclaimed over and inevitably assessed and dissected.

She was relieved, in a way, that her friends were all away or busy with their own lives because for once she just wanted to enjoy her own.

With a smile, she turned off the lights and headed downstairs. An hour later she was heading into Wychwood's parish church with Tina, the familiar smell of dust and candle wax, mixed with fresh holly and evergreen, bringing a rush of childhood memories.

"How lovely," Tina murmured as they took their seats in a pew near the front. "They decorate the church so beautifully."

Olivia glanced around the church as the rest of the pews began to fill up, and several people whom she'd met through the tea shop events smiled or waved at her. She did the same back, heartened that after two years she was finally feeling more part of the village. Perhaps some things just took time.

Then the service started, and the orchestra music to accompany the carol singing soared to the rafters, breathtaking and beautiful. Olivia let the music flow over her as a deep peace settled in her soul. She was thankful for so much—not just Simon coming into her life, but for her friends, her shop, her lovely, loving mum. Yes, life could be hard, and she knew there were some definite challenges ahead. But it was also good, and she savoured each moment like the gift she knew it was.

Later in the service the lights were dimmed and candles passed around as Simon performed a solo on the cello for

"Silent Night," everyone singing along softly. Olivia watched as a hundred different candle flames flickered throughout the church, and she closed her eyes to offer a silent prayer of gratitude.

The challenges, she discovered, came sooner than she might have wished. After enjoying yet more mulled wine—it seemed no one offered anything else for the entire month of December—and a shop-bought mince pie, they all walked back to the flat. Olivia served up the fish pie while Simon and Tina chatted, and then they played a few hands of bridge afterwards while sipping thimbleful-sized glasses of sherry.

And then her mum got confused. It happened so suddenly, Olivia didn't feel prepared. Foolishly she expected some warning, a buzzer to go off, some signal. Instead they were chatting one minute and the next her mum was looking up from her hand of cards and blinking at them both in confusion.

"Mum…?" Olivia asked, not twigging what was going on. "How many do you want to bid?"

"Bid?" Her mother looked completely blank, sounding as if she'd never heard the word before. Then she turned to Simon. "I'm sorry, do I know you?"

"Mum—" Olivia's voice, sharp and loud, cut through the silence before she could stop herself.

But then Simon answered easily, "I'm Simon, Olivia's friend. We're playing bridge."

"Bridge...?" Still her mother looked uncomprehending, and worse, fearful.

"Yes, you love bridge, Mum. You've been playing it for ages." Even though she tried not to, Olivia couldn't keep an odd, wheedling note from entering her voice. She felt panicky, which she knew wouldn't help, but it was as if her mother had forgotten everything in the space of a few seconds—as if her brain had been wiped clean, like a slate.

"I'm sorry..." Tina put her cards down, shaking her head. "I don't know what I'm doing here."

Olivia tried to suppress the panic rising in her like a tide, blotting out rational thought. She knew arguing with her mum wouldn't help, and neither would insisting on the facts as she knew them. The trouble was, she didn't know what to do. She hadn't done enough research yet, about how to handle moments like these. She hadn't expected them to come so soon.

"It's all right, Tina," Simon said, his voice calm and reassuring. "It's Christmas Eve, and you're in the flat above the tea shop with your daughter, Olivia." She blinked at him uncertainly while Olivia tried to swallow past the lump forming in her throat. "Would you like to go outside, get some air and clear your head? Or if you're tired, perhaps you could go to bed? It is getting late."

Tina shook her head slowly. "I don't know...everything feels grey...like there's nothing there." Her hands knotted in her lap, her face creased with both concentration and fear.

"It's okay, Mum," Olivia said as steadily as she could. "It will come back. Maybe getting some rest is a good idea. It's been a long day."

"All right." She rose from the table a bit unsteadily, and Simon hurried to help her. Olivia took her arm and guided her towards the spare bedroom, fetching her nightclothes and wash bag. "Can you manage? Or would you like some help...?"

"I can manage," Tina said with a kind of chilly dignity, taking the things from Olivia. "I'm sorry. I don't know what happened."

Olivia tried to smile, although she still felt near tears. "It's okay, Mum."

"We were playing bridge?" She sounded wondering.

"Yes, you like bridge." She hesitated, unsure if she should press the issue or not. "It doesn't matter now, Mum," she finally said. "Get some sleep."

Twenty minutes later Tina was settled into bed; Olivia had tucked her in like a child, sitting on the edge of the bed until she'd drifted off.

Back in the sitting room, she glanced helplessly at Simon and he just opened his arms. Olivia walked into them, grateful for the comfort. Thankful there was someone in her life to be there for her, a comforting shoulder, a steady presence.

"That's never happened before," she mumbled against his chest as his arms closed around her and drew her close. "I mean, she's been forgetful and things, but not like that."

"I'm sorry."

"You seemed like you knew what to do."

"My grandmother had Alzheimer's. The doctor told us to give her the facts of a situation when she was confused, as well as options. Help her to feel in control."

"Thank you for doing that. Clearly I need to do more research." She pressed her cheek against his shoulder, breathing in his familiar, woodsy scent, savouring the connection. "I suppose I've been fooling myself a little bit, because she's seemed okay these last few days. I didn't think it was bad as…as that."

"Like with most things, there are good days and bad days." He hesitated, and once again Olivia had the sense he wanted to say something more. She lifted her head.

"Simon…?"

He smiled and touched her cheek. "You have a lot to deal with, Olivia."

"And I'm so glad you're here to help me with it. I don't know what I would do without you," she confessed, and then wondered if she was being too honest, too needy. "I feel badly for bringing you into all this, though."

"This is life, though, isn't it?" Simon said with a sad smile. "The good and the bad."

"Yes, but it's a lot to deal with, especially in a new relationship." She bit her lip. "I'm sorry."

"You don't need to be sorry."

"Still…"

"I mean it." He sounded so serious, but also a little bleak. Olivia feared the mood had inexplicably altered, and not just because of her mum. She wasn't sure how to get it back.

Then Simon kissed her softly on the lips. "But let's not worry about all that now. Each day has its own trouble, right? And remember, it's almost Christmas."

THE NEXT MORNING Olivia woke up, blinking fuzzily, to see big, fat snowflakes drifting down outside her window. She let out a little yelp of happy surprise, and then heard her phone ping. She grabbed it from the bedside table and saw a photo of Simon's little garden at Willoughby Close, covered in a very thin layer of snow. *White Christmas!*

He'd been living there for the last few days, with nothing but a mattress on the floor and a few boxes of possessions. No wonder he was spending all his time with her…although Olivia knew it was more than that. She laughed aloud and sent back a photo of the snowflakes outside her window. *See you soon?*

Be there in ten.

Still smiling, she got out of bed. Tina was still sleeping and so Olivia took the opportunity to shower and prep the roast dinner they'd be having later. She also put her presents under the tree—a book of sudoku puzzles for her mum that were meant to help cognitive function, as well as a deliciously soft cashmere throw, since her flat was a bit cold. For Simon she'd bought a new Aran jumper in a deep hunter's green, since his old one had a seriously unravelled hem. Excitement mixed with a few nerves fluttered in her stomach as she thought of him opening it.

"Good morning." Tina emerged from the bedroom in her dressing gown, looking a lot more like herself.

"Morning, Mum. How are you feeling?"

"I'm well, thank you. Shall I make coffee?" As her mum bustled towards the kitchen, Olivia realised she had no recollection of her blank memory moment last night, and she decided that was okay. They could just go with it. Take the good moments as they came, along with the bad.

Simon arrived a short while later, and they all had coffee and croissants before opening their presents. Tina was thrilled with both the book and the throw, and Olivia held her breath while Simon opened her present, letting out a little sigh of relief when he exclaimed how delighted he was with it, and in typical Simon fashion, insisted on putting it on right then and there.

Then it was her turn, and she opened a flat, rectangular-shaped present from Simon, wondering what it was.

"It's lovely," she exclaimed when she saw the buttery-soft leather cover. She flipped through the pages, noting the plastic pockets for photos and the blank, lined pages.

"It's for your recipes," Simon explained. "Since you've made up so many wonderful ones for the cupcakes. I thought you could put them down for posterity."

"I love it, truly." She was so touched he'd got something properly thoughtful, and not just the typical perfume or scarf. "It's perfect."

And the rest of the day was perfect, as well—Tina was in good form, and Simon carried them along with his humour and boyish enthusiasm for everything, from being in charge of the Yorkshire pudding batter, to fashioning odd shapes from the linen napkins. He introduced them to a game from his own family—putting an After Eight mint on your forehead and trying to get it into your mouth without hands, by simply wiggling your eyebrows and mouth.

Olivia's sides ached from laughing and melted chocolate streaked her cheeks as she finally managed to nab the mint and munch it triumphantly. Simon, of course, was a dab hand—no pun intended—at it, managing to get mint from brow to mouth in a mere nine seconds.

"You could be in the *Guinness World Records* book," Olivia marvelled while he shrugged modestly.

All in all, Olivia couldn't remember the last time she'd had so much fun, or felt so happy. As they clinked glasses of Prosecco over the remains of the turkey, she exchanged smiles with both Tina and Simon, thinking if she could keep this moment intact in her memory forever, holding it in her hands like one of the glass baubles on the tree, she would be perfectly content—no matter what happened or went wrong.

Chapter Fourteen

*A*LZHEIMER'S. THE WORD was familiar and yet utterly strange. Olivia sat in the doctor's office at the memory clinic, after Tina had gone through a memory test and the results of her blood tests, and now they were listening to the expected and yet suddenly startling result.

"There's no definitive test or diagnosis," the doctor explained gently. "Only ruling out other options. We can refer you for a CT scan of the brain, which may help, but judging from what I've read in your file and seen today, I think this is the most likely outcome."

Tina nodded stoically, her chin tilted at a proud angle. "I expected as much."

The doctor glanced at Olivia. "There is loads of support available here in Witney," she said. "Groups and memory clinics and we can look into different medications and foods that help alleviate some of the symptoms." She placed several colourful brochures on the desk in front of them. "You can read through the literature and we'll schedule an appointment for you to come back in a few weeks, and discuss any questions or concerns, as well as how you want to go forward."

"There's no fighting it, you know," Tina told Olivia once they were back in her flat, and Olivia was putting on the kettle for a much-needed cup of tea. "It's not like cancer. It's not something you can beat."

"But you don't have to give up, Mum." Olivia felt shaky, even though the diagnosis had been entirely expected. She'd texted Simon to let him know the news, but he hadn't responded yet.

"I'm not giving up. I'll eat the superfoods and take the supplements or whatever medication will help. And I'll enjoy my life while I have it. But I just want you to be prepared, Olivia. Decline is inevitable."

"Oh, Mum." Impulsively Olivia threw her arms around her mother, hugging her tight, wanting to imbue her with her love and strength. "I love you so much, you know. I don't tell you often enough…"

"Yes, you do, darling," Tina said gently. "But you can always tell me again, just as I'll tell you. I love you. That will never change. No matter how much I forget." Tina's lips trembled. "Even if I forget who I am, or who you are. Please know that, darling. Know I'll always, always love you. I'll always be proud of who you are, all the things you've done. You're my brightest star, Olivia. Never forget that, even if I do."

Tears ran down Olivia's cheeks and she nodded as she

took a shuddering breath, not trusting herself to speak without breaking down into sobs. Tina returned her affection with a tight hug and then stepped back as the kettle began to whistle. "Now enough of this nonsense," she said briskly. "I'm not dead yet, so there's no need to talk in epitaphs. Why don't you ring Simon and we'll play a hand of bridge?"

Simon didn't pick up, however, and so they played with just the two of them, before Olivia headed back to Wychwood as dusk settled over the fields. She hadn't seen Simon for two days, which really wasn't that much, but she was starting to feel the teensiest bit nervous about his radio silence. It was by far the longest they'd gone without talking in admittedly, only ten days. But it had been an amazing, intense ten days.

On Boxing Day they'd had leftovers for lunch and gone for a lovely, long walk through snowy fields along the Lea, and then come back and watched all the special Christmas season telly.

Then yesterday he'd said he needed to organise his new home, and since the subtext seemed to be he was too busy to spend time with her, Olivia let it be. They didn't have to live in each other's pockets, after all. These last days had been magical, but Olivia was sensible enough—or so she told herself—to accept that they hadn't been actual reality. Real life had to intrude at some point, and so now it was. They'd learn to live in the real world, not some snowy, Christmassy idyll.

Still, as she arrived back at Tea on the Lea, Dr Jekyll me-owing resentfully at being left alone for so long, she wondered again at Simon's uncharacteristic silence. He hadn't replied to any of her three texts, or answered her two calls. She was reluctant to text or call yet again, and clutter up his phone with her clinginess. Perhaps he'd lost his mobile…but then wouldn't he have let her know? He'd known she was taking her mum to the doctor's today. They'd made plans to be together afterwards, and he'd acknowledged how she might be a bit shaky. So where was he now?

Restless, Olivia fed Dr Jekyll and made herself a mug of soup, pacing the flat as she sipped it and trying not to feel anxious. A few unanswered texts were hardly the end of the world, and Simon could have any number of reasons not to respond: a family emergency…a lost phone…or perhaps he was just tired, and he'd had a nap all afternoon. Or maybe he was busy with DIY stuff, and hadn't had a chance to look at his phone. She was being ridiculous. Of course she was.

But when he hadn't called by ten o'clock that night, Olivia started to feel properly frightened. What if he'd had a fall, alone in number four? What if he was lying at the bottom of the stairs with a broken leg? She tortured herself with various scenarios before she threw on her parka and boots and headed outside. The night was black and starless, the pavements icy, the air sharp and cold, as she headed down the deserted high street towards Willoughby Manor.

She was probably overreacting hugely, and Simon might start to wonder if she was some kind of sick bunny boiler, going out to check on him late at night, peering in his windows. In fact, Olivia nearly turned around at the thought—what on earth was she *doing*?

But then she thought of Simon lying on the floor, bloody and unconscious, and she kept walking.

Willoughby Close looked empty and forlorn as she came into the courtyard. Simon's car wasn't parked there, which surprised her. Where was he, if not at home? She peeked in the windows but the curtains were drawn and she couldn't see anything. After a few indecisive moments she crept away, and spent a restless night wondering where he was and what he was doing, trying not to feed her ever-growing fear that something was wrong.

When her phone pinged early the next morning Olivia scrabbled on her bedside table for it, only to sigh in disappointment when she saw it was Alice, asking her if she and Simon wanted to come over for drinks on New Year's Eve. Since she wasn't sure where Simon was and was starting to doubt the nature of their relationship, she decided to answer it later.

After a restorative shower and a large cup of coffee, Olivia was starting to feel more like herself. Simon would almost certainly get in touch today, with a completely reasonable explanation, and she would laugh at her paranoia and never,

ever tell him how freaked out she'd become.

She spent the morning tidying the flat and then taking down the Christmas decorations in the shop, getting everything ready for a reopen on January second. She made a shopping list to restock, and fiddled around with some new recipes…checking her phone every few minutes all the while.

In the afternoon she drove into Witney to check on her mum, and they went for a walk around town before having tea at a cute little shop in the Woolgate Centre. When she got back home in the early evening, Simon still hadn't been in touch and she was starting to panic properly, forgetting all the resolutions she'd made about keeping her cool.

Something *had* to be wrong. He wouldn't just go quiet on her like this, not without sending a single text. That wasn't like him at all, and yet Olivia was forced to acknowledge that she had only known Simon for a handful of weeks, and they'd been dating for less than that. Yes, things had become intense quickly, and she *felt* as if she knew him…but did she really? What if he was one of those serial monogamists who loved the initial rush of a relationship, but then scarpered off? What if he was like her dad, someone who stayed for the short term but couldn't handle the long haul?

Fear wound everything inside her tighter and tighter, until she couldn't think properly at all. She felt as if she could barely function, and she hated that already he'd affected her so much. She was more than halfway to falling in love with him, and perhaps he'd already broken her heart. What else was she to think?

She called him again, leaving a voicemail she hoped was upbeat but feared sounded frantic, and then settled in for a night of watching telly alone—something that wouldn't have bothered her before, but everything had changed with Simon. She wanted so much more out of life now. She wanted to be with him, and this sudden silence from him was making her realise how much she cared about him…and how afraid she was that she'd already lost him.

Just like her dad. Issues she'd never even realised she had suddenly swamped her—because as she sat there alone, staring at the TV, she knew part of her had been waiting for this all along. To be left behind. To be discarded, because she wasn't important enough to somebody. She never had been. Still a supporting role in her life, she thought gloomily as she dug in the freezer for a pint of mint chocolate ice cream. It was time to pull out all the comfort stops.

By New Year's Eve Olivia was feeling utterly despondent. It had been five days since she'd seen Simon, four since she'd heard from him, and even though she kept telling herself that this still didn't have to be a big deal, in her heart she knew it was. Simon wasn't the kind of man to not be in touch…except it seemed he was. It had to be the end of everything, because what else could it be? She had no other answers, no possibilities that didn't border on the utterly ludicrous.

She texted Alice to say they'd have to give New Year's Eve a miss, and spent the last day of the year binging on a boxed set and yet another tub of ice cream, feeling utterly miserable. At least Dr Jekyll was in a friendly mood, sprawled in her lap, his purring as loud as the motor of the car.

A few minutes later, however, determined tapping at the door downstairs had Olivia upending a highly offended cat from her lap. She hurried downstairs, so sure, so absolutely *certain* that Simon would be standing there, with his colourful scarf and unruly hair and wry grin—and a credible, completely understandable reason why he'd been AWOL for five days. Except he wasn't.

"Bella…?" Olivia said slowly as she opened the door to Simon's sister. They hadn't officially met yet, but obviously Bella knew who she was, to be here at nearly ten o'clock on New Year's Eve—and Olivia knew who she was, from the concert in the church what felt like a lifetime ago now. "Is everything okay?" Her heart lurched with fear. "Is Simon…?"

Bella looked weary and careworn, swathed in a thick winter coat. "May I come in?"

"Yes, of course. I thought you were still visiting your in-laws…"

"I was, but when Simon didn't answer his phone or respond to my texts, I started to get worried. I drove home this afternoon."

Olivia's stomach freefell towards her toes. Oh no. *Oh no...* "Worried..." she whispered, barely managing to get the one word out. "What... Why?"

Bella sighed heavily, raking a hand through her hair the same way Simon so often did. "You don't...you don't know about Simon, do you?"

"Know what?" Olivia asked numbly. She was getting really tired of people knowing more about Simon than she did. She wanted to know him completely. She wanted to be given the chance. "I know about how he got fired from his teaching job in London..." she began, trailing off uncertainly. She knew about his brother dying, and the effect it had had on him. She knew he was funny and sweet and sometimes a little bit sad. She knew a lot, and yet right now she had a feeling there was something she didn't know. Something big.

"Simon suffers from depression," Bella said quietly. "Quite serious depression. He's struggled with it off and on since his teens, but it got worse after Andrew died. He was hospitalised for a short while, about a year and a half ago."

"Oh." Olivia's mind whirled emptily. She tried to organise her thoughts coherently, but her mind felt buzzing and blank. She hadn't expected something like this, and yet now she wondered if she should have. Was there any way she could have known?

"He doesn't like talking about it," Bella continued, "doesn't like people knowing, because he feels like it colours their perception of him. I wouldn't normally tell you, but I know how much he's come to care about you, and I think it's wrong that he's hiding this from you…considering." She let out a long, low breath. "He's had a relapse over the last few days. I found him at Willoughby Close, lying in bed, practically comatose, not speaking, eating, anything. It's how he gets sometimes. I've brought him back to my home, and he's doing a bit better. He's showered, at least." She tried for a wry smile like Simon's but her eyes were full of sorrow—and fear. "I don't know what to do. He's been on medication but he stopped it recently, and he says he doesn't want to take it again. He won't talk to me, and I don't even know what set him off, if anything set him off. Sometimes it just happens."

Bella blinked back tears. "I'm not trying to rat him out, honestly. I'm trying to help him, and this is the only way I know how. I thought maybe if he saw you…if you talked to him…"

Olivia's mind suddenly sprung into gear. She still had a lot to think about and process, but if Simon needed her help, any help, then she was ready to give it. More than ready.

"Shall I come with you now?"

Bella nodded as she wiped a tear from her cheek. "Yes, please. He's doing a bit better than he was…like I said, he's showered and he ate a bit of the soup I gave him. He's not as bad as he was, you know, before."

Olivia nodded, even though she didn't really understand about *before*. She'd never struggled with this kind of depression herself, and already she felt out of her depth. She didn't know what to do, but she still wanted to try.

"I hope he'll want to talk to you," Bella said. "But if he doesn't…"

"If he doesn't want me there, I'll go," Olivia reassured her. "I won't be offended. I understand…he's not quite himself."

"Except he would tell you this *is* himself." Bella sighed. "At least, he would say that in the moment. It's so hard on him, Olivia. He hates that he struggles with this. It feels like weakness to him, but it really isn't."

"I know." She knew that much, at least, about mental health issues, but not much more. And yet…things were starting to click into place.

She remembered now what Simon had said about good days and bad days. About the value of medication and diagnosis. She recalled how Bella had hugged Simon after the Advent concert, and realised how significant it must have been for Simon to have been playing again, *living* again. And she thought of the days, early in their acquaintance, when he hadn't come in for a cupcake, when he'd made what seemed like an excuse. *Good and bad days.* Perhaps she should have seen it, guessed it, considering the trauma he'd experienced with his brother's death, the sensitivity he clearly showed to other people and to life itself. But she hadn't. She'd been so concerned about her own feelings, caught up in her own fears.

"Shall we go?" she asked, and Bella nodded.

They drove to a modest semi-detached house on the other side of Wychwood, the part Harriet had jokingly called "the rougher side" even though there was nothing rough whatsoever about the houses there, most of which cost close to half a million pounds.

Olivia thought about making small talk, but she couldn't think of anything to say, and Bella seemed too tense and unhappy to talk.

"I hope I'm doing the right thing," she said as they got out of the car. "It's not my secret to share, I know that." She looked so worried and miserable that Olivia wanted to hug her.

"I care about Simon a lot," she said quietly. "And I mean *a lot*. I'm glad to know what's going on. In some ways, it's a relief." Just as her mother's diagnosis had been. Knowing was always better than not knowing...and fearing what you didn't know.

"A relief?" Bella looked confused.

"When you knocked on the door, I was eating my body weight in ice cream because I was sure Simon had gone off me."

"I don't think he has," Bella said with a small smile. "In fact, I'm sure he hasn't. He's told me about you...about what he feels for you..."

"Good." Olivia smiled back, her heart feeling impossibly lighter despite all the challenges still ahead. "That's all that matters, then."

"I'm glad you think that," Bella said seriously, her smile fading. "And I hope you continue to do so."

A few minutes later Olivia was standing in front of a closed bedroom door, tapping on it gently. "Simon…?" she called. "It's Olivia." There was no answer. "Simon…" Uncertainly she pushed the door open, blinking in the gloom. She could make out a shape on the bed—Simon, sitting back against the pillows, his arms folded, his gaze distant, a cup of tea going cold on the table next to him. He didn't speak.

Olivia stepped into the room, praying she was strong enough for this. She hadn't known how to handle her mum's memory lapses, and she wasn't sure how to handle this situation, either, but she knew she loved her mum and she was falling in love with Simon and surely, *surely* that was what mattered?

"Simon." She perched on the edge of the bed, gazing at him in tender concern. He was freshly showered and dressed in a frayed jumper and old cords, looking so wonderfully familiar and yet also so strange, for there was a vacant and desolate look in his usually glinting eyes that made her ache. "Oh, Simon." She covered his hand with her own, having no idea what to say but simply wanting to be there for him.

"I'm sorry." He spoke the two words so quietly she almost didn't hear them.

"You don't need to be sorry, Simon. Of course you

don't."

"I...I never wanted you to see me like this."

Tears pricked Olivia's eyes. "Good and bad days," she reminded him softly. "Just like you said."

"Yes, but...I like me on the good days." He let out a shuddering breath. "Not like this. Never like this."

"You were going to have to tell me sometime," she said quietly. "Weren't you?"

"I suppose. I hoped...I hoped I wouldn't have to. It doesn't...it doesn't always hit me like this, you know. I can go months...even more...without feeling this way."

"What happened?" Olivia asked, unsure if that was the right question. "I mean, did something happen? To...set you off?" She was fumbling in the dark; she'd never dealt with depression before, not like this, and she was afraid to use the wrong words, ask the wrong questions.

"No," Simon said on a sigh. "Nothing did. At least, not that I know of. Sometimes it can be something on a subconscious level: a smell, a sudden memory, anything. And sometimes it's nothing at all. I just wake up one morning and I feel it coming, like a fog I can see rolling in, and there's nothing I can do to stop it."

"And is that what happened this time?"

"Yes, more or less. I was organising the house and then I woke up on the twenty-eighth and I felt as if I could barely get out of bed. As if there was no point in living."

Olivia caught her breath at the pain in his voice, a pain

she felt in herself. This man she loved was hurting so very much. "I'm so sorry."

"It's not your fault. If it's anyone's, it's—"

"No, Simon, it's not yours," Olivia said fiercely. "I may not know a lot about depression, but at least I know that." She stroked his hair, and he closed his eyes.

"What did Bella tell you?"

"Only that you suffered from depression."

He opened his eyes and looked at her directly. "Did she tell you I was hospitalised?"

"After your brother's death, yes."

"Does that scare you off?"

"No," Olivia answered honestly, "but it scares me a little. Because...because I want to be able to help you, and I don't know if it's the sort of thing where I can."

"You have helped me, Olivia. Being with you...these last few weeks...it made me feel as if I've finally beaten this thing...which is why having it come at me again is so...so bloody difficult." He pressed his lips together, shaking his head. "I know depression doesn't work that way, that it doesn't follow a course, and sometimes there's no rhyme or reason, but I still convince myself that there is. That things will change."

"I don't know too much about depression," Olivia said slowly, "but I do know it's real, not something you can just make yourself get over, or slap a smile on like a plaster. Be kind to yourself, Simon. Be forgiving."

"Even though I watched my brother die?" He let out a shuddering sigh. "Sorry."

"You don't need to be sorry about this. Ever." Olivia spoke the words fiercely, and Simon gave her the barest flicker of a smile.

"You are the best thing that's ever happened to me," he said in a low voice. "Truly."

"And you're the best thing that has ever happened to me. This doesn't change that at all. What kind of person would I be, to only take the good days and not the bad? That's not…that's not what love is."

He turned to look at her, his eyes huge and dark. "Do you mean that?"

"Yes," she whispered, her heart beating hard. "I really do."

"Because I think I love you, Olivia."

"You only think?" she dared to tease.

"I know, and maybe that's part of it all. Of this. I'm scared to let you in, to let you see my darkness, especially when we've only known each other a short while."

"And I've been scared to let you in," Olivia admitted with a wobbly laugh. "Because I haven't let many people into my life. Maybe it has to do with my dad walking out, or maybe it's just the way I'm wired. But it's the truth. This is just as scary for me as it is for you, Simon."

"I'm glad, in a way. I wouldn't want to be the only one who is struggling, the dead weight in the relationship."

"You aren't, I promise."

He was silent, his gaze seeming to turn inward. Olivia stayed where she sat, waiting. Knowing none of this was easy, and Simon could hardly snap out of whatever he was feeling, no matter what he wished for.

He closed his eyes, leaning his head back against the bedstead as he let out a long, low breath. "How was your mum's appointment?" he asked after a long, silent moment.

"It was okay." Olivia knew how much it cost him, to ask about her mum when he was hurting so much himself, and she loved him all the more for it. "We'll get there," she said, and Simon opened his eyes to give her a long, meaningful look.

"Yes," he agreed. "We will. But it won't be easy."

"The best things in life aren't."

He shook his head, his expression closing up once again. "You don't even know what you're agreeing to, Olivia. What you're letting yourself in for."

"No," Olivia agreed steadily, more sure of this than anything she'd been sure of in her life, "but then neither do you. No one does. This isn't some social contract, Simon, weighing the pros and the cons. This is me, all in for you, and you all in for me. That's the kind of relationship I want, not some balancing of the scales."

He stared at her for another long moment, his eyes full of both torment and hope. "I don't think I love you," he finally said hoarsely. "I know I do."

Olivia gazed down at this man who had come so suddenly and wonderfully into her life, this man who loved her. "And I know I love you," she said, meaning it utterly.

Outside, the church bells began to ring in the new year.

Epilogue

Three months later

"WHO IS THAT?" Olivia peered outside the window of Number Four, Willoughby Close, as a navy-blue sports convertible sped into the courtyard and parked in front of the first cottage in the close.

Simon looked up from his hand of cards. "I believe it's my new neighbour. Tina, it's your bid."

Olivia watched as a slim young woman with glossy chestnut hair marched up to number one and unlocked the door with brisk efficiency, a posh-looking leather messenger bag slung over one shoulder.

"She looks very Londonish," Olivia remarked, and Simon raised his eyebrows.

"Perhaps that's because she comes from London. She's Henry Trent's executive assistant."

"Is she! Alice never said anything about it." But then Alice had been busy lately, managing the charitable foundation she and Henry had started. And Olivia had been busy, as well…

She turned away from the window to smile at Simon and Tina, both seated at the kitchen table for their weekly Sunday afternoon game of bridge. The consultant at the memory clinic had encouraged Tina to keep playing cards, as it helped with cognitive function, and the new medication she was on had helped a bit as well. Simon was on new medication as well, a low dosage that had kept him on more of an even keel, although he still had good and bad days…just as everyone did, in one way or another.

The last three months had been challenging in some ways, but they had also been wonderful. Unbelievably wonderful, full of discovery and fun and love—lots of love. Every day felt like an adventure, and after living life on the sidelines, voluntarily cast in a supporting role in everyone else's lives, Olivia was glad to feel like the star of her own story. She'd gone after love and she'd found it…with Simon.

Now crocuses and daffodils dotted the wolds, and Olivia was starting on a spring promotion of Easter-themed cupcakes, complete with baby chick toppers, as well as several orders for wedding cakes. Business at Tea on the Lea wasn't exactly booming, but it was doing well enough, and that was fine. She had more important things to think about, anyway.

In the last few months Olivia had joined the village's bridge society, and had also started a baking club for kids Mallory's age. So far she had eight girls coming in on a Wednesday afternoon. After living in Wychwood-on-Lea for over two years, Olivia was finally starting to feel a part of things…and so was Simon.

"Your bid, love," he said with a smile and, with her heart full, Olivia spared one last glance for the new neighbour before rejoining them at the table.

"You'll have to have her over for drinks," she said as she picked up her cards.

"You mean we will," Simon corrected. "I couldn't do it without you."

"And I couldn't either," Olivia agreed softly.

They shared a lingering, knowing look before Tina interjected briskly, "Now I bid four hearts. Let's get in the game, everyone!"

The End

If you enjoyed this return to Willoughby Close,
look for three more stories about the new residents of
Willoughby Close in 2019!

The Willoughby Close series

Discover the lives and loves of the residents of Willoughby Close

The four occupants of Willoughby Close are utterly different and about to become best friends, each in search of her own happy ending as they navigate the treacherous waters of modern womanhood in the quirky yet beautiful village of Shipstow, nestled in the English Cotswolds...

Book 1: *A Cotswold Christmas*

Book 2: *Meet Me at Willoughby Close*

Book 3: *Find me at Willoughby Close*

Book 4: *Kiss Me at Willoughby Close*

Book 5: *Marry Me at Willoughby Close*

Available now at your favorite online retailer!

About the Author

After spending three years as a diehard New Yorker, **Kate Hewitt** now lives in the Lake District in England with her husband, their five children, and a Golden Retriever. She enjoys such novel things as long country walks and chatting with people in the street, and her children love the freedom of village life—although she often has to ring four or five people to figure out where they've gone off to.

She writes women's fiction as well as contemporary romance under the name Kate Hewitt, and whatever the genre she enjoys delivering a compelling and intensely emotional story.

You can find out more about Katharine on her website at kate-hewitt.com.

Thank you for reading

Cupcakes for Christmas

If you enjoyed this book, you can find more from all our great authors at TulePublishing.com, or from your favorite online retailer.

TULE
PUBLISHING

Made in United States
North Haven, CT
19 January 2023

31236781R00129